Murder (maybe) at Martyn Manor

Copyright © 2025 by Mershon Niesner.

All rights reserved. No part of this book may be used
or reproduced in any manner whatsoever without
prior written consent of the author, except as provided
by the United States of America copyright law.

All the characters in this book are fictional.
Any resemblance to an actual person is unintentional.

ISBN: 978-0-9743076-8-8 (Paperback)
ISBN: 978-0-9743076-9-5 (eBook)

Library of Congress Control Number: 2025908164

Cover and layout design by Lance Buckley

Murder (maybe) at Martyn Manor

Martyn Manor Mystery #2

MERSHON NIESNER

In loving memory of my BFF

Nancy Giese

3/11/35 - 8/1/25

Books By Mershon

Mom's Gone, Now What?

The Bookmaker's Wife

Angie, The Bee Lady

It's (Mostly) Good To Be Martha
Martyn Manor Mystery #1

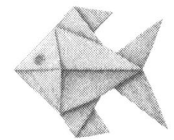

Chapter One

New Year's Day is traditionally a time to make resolutions or consider goals for the future. I, on the other hand, was contemplating whether or not this year would be my last.

My dear dad died at ninety-two but he always said, "Martha, you don't smoke, you don't carouse, you rarely drink so I have no doubt you'll live to be a hundred." I wondered if his prediction would come true.

Although I celebrated my ninety-first birthday last October, I was in the habit of thinking a year ahead so my future age wouldn't come as a shock. Consequently, as I sat on my recliner looking out the window of my assisted-living apartment at the cold, bleak January morning in Poughkeepsie, New York, I was already in my dad's ninety-two-year-old shoes.

I'd made an effort to live my life to the fullest and, knock on wood, experienced mostly good health. But I was a realist. As my dad used to say, "You can't kid a kidder." Death was just around the corner, and I wanted to be as mentally prepared as possible for the inevitable.

Last October when I attended my granddaughter Susan's wedding, I truly thought that perfect day was destined to be my last. My three children, Richard, Ruth, and Elizabeth; three grandchildren, Susan, Barbara, and Rich; and two great-grands, Marti and David, were together for the first time. Following the ceremony, I dined on puff pastries filled with crab, a succulent duck à l'orange, and good French wine. Then after a brief twirl around the dance floor, I'd fallen asleep curled up behind my dear friend, Harold Lancaster.

It was the perfect night to have a heart attack and die in my sleep but it obviously wasn't in the cards because here I was two and a half months later, contemplating what was next for me in a fresh new year.

When I heard a knock on my door, I knew it was Harold coming to fetch me for breakfast. I was still able to live alone in my apartment but due to a lack of oxygen to parts of my aged brain, I frequently had trouble navigating the halls of my facility as the day drew to a close. So, Harold kindly escorted me to and from dinner and, on special occasions like New Year's Day, he joined me for breakfast.

I opened my door to Harold's smiling face. "Good morning, Martha. Happy New Year!"

Harold hadn't aged much in the last year. He still had slightly rounded broad shoulders, a paunch which was mitigated by his ever-present jumpsuits, thinning white hair, and glasses. Since getting a pacemaker last year, he was rather robust for a ninety-three-year-old.

After I gave Harold a peck on the cheek, we walked into the hall, then I closed and locked my door. "Happy New Year to you, too. You look chipper today. What's up?"

"Nothing in particular. Just thinking that even though I thought I was a goner last year, here I am, escorting my lovely lady to breakfast."

Harold gave me a side-eye glance. I knew he was wondering what my response would be to his "my lovely lady" comment. I wasn't one who wanted to be possessed. My independent streak was well-known by family and friends. It had gotten me into a few scrapes in the past, but I wasn't ready to let it go. I liked being my own person, even if I did need to be escorted to meals and my clothes closet was arranged in categories so I wouldn't show up dressed for dinner in polka dots and plaid.

I ignored the possessive comment thinking there were worse things than being someone's lovely lady. In fact, since Harold and I started spending time together every day, the idea of being his lady was becoming more appealing all the time. "Are you making any resolutions?" I asked him.

He barked out a short laugh. "Are you kidding me? My main goal is to continue walking you to dinner."

"That's not a very ambitious goal for a retired Army Colonel."

Harold corrected me. "Lieutenant Colonel, Martha."

I rolled my eyes at him. He ignored my gesture. "I'm not exactly planning missions in the swamps of Vietnam or resolving to run a marathon. Hell, I'm just happy when I can get to the bathroom in the middle of the night without tripping over a cord."

I couldn't help but chuckle. Like me, Harold was a realist. That's one reason we got along so well. We didn't kid ourselves or each other.

Our conversation halted as we walked along the cafeteria line and gathered our breakfast items. In recent weeks, I'd deviated from my usual Grape-Nuts cereal, branching out to an occasional English muffin with chunky peanut butter and whatever fresh fruit looked appetizing. I was tempted by the smell of crisp bacon but refrained.

After we sat down, I asked Harold about his woodworking projects, thinking the question might bring us back to our earlier conversation. I was taken aback by his response.

"Remember Joey Russo, the lock-picker guy?"

"My mind may be hazy at times but I certainly couldn't forget him."

It irritated me that Harold felt the need to reiterate something so important from my past. He probably thought my memory was even worse than it was.

"So, what about Joey?" I prompted.

"Well, since he's under house arrest, I've been keeping my eye on him. He's usually in the shop when I'm there and lately he's been acting suspicious."

My ears perked up. I couldn't help it. In my advanced age I'd become a bit of a sleuth, and starting the year off with a new mystery to solve was right up my alley. In the past, I'd fashioned myself after Queen Latifah, star of the television series *The Equalizer*. Now I was thinking more along the lines of Kathy Bates in the new *Matlock* series. At seventy-seven, she was closer to my age. Even though she played a lawyer on the TV show, she was constantly in investigative mode. "Suspicious how?" I asked, trying hard to keep the excitement out of my voice.

Harold added blackberry jam to his toast. Patience wasn't a virtue I possessed but since it was morning, my patience bucket was full, so I waited quietly for him to respond.

"Instead of making things out of wood, he seems to be experimenting with metal scraps."

I nonchalantly took a sip of my green tea with lemon. "Experimenting how?"

"He's cutting out odd designs with tin snips but I don't see anything taking shape." Harold forked in a bite of cheesy omelet.

"Do you think he's making something that will violate his parole?"

"Maybe, but who's to know? It's not like anyone's watching him in this place. He meets with his parole officer once a month who, from what I hear, pats him on the head and that's it." Harold sipped his coffee then looked over at me. "I see that gleam in your eye."

I tried to show him an innocent smile but Harold knew me too well to be hoodwinked. "Who, me?"

Harold impolitely pointed his finger. "Yes, you. Don't let my casual observation about Joey give you any ideas, Martha. You said your private investigator days were over after your participation in that murder case on the cruise."

He was correct. I had said that fifteen months ago when I went on a Transatlantic cruise with my granddaughter and witnessed a murder on the ship, but I was getting the itch again. Still, I nodded in the affirmative. It was just a little white lie. I didn't even say it out loud. Instead, I said, "Well, when he was arrested, they took away all of his tools and skeleton keys. Maybe he's attempting to make new ones. I think you should ask about his project. That's what a friend would do."

Harold's forehead scrunched into a frown so I quickly added, "What's the harm? He doesn't know you had anything to do with his arrest. He thinks you're his friend."

I knew I challenged Harold's patience, but somehow he stuck around anyway. Besides, given our past experiences, I believed he secretly liked solving mysteries as much as I did. He certainly got excited when he participated in The Purse Snatcher Operation a few years ago.

Before finishing his omelet, Harold said "maybe" under his breath. He probably thought I didn't hear him.

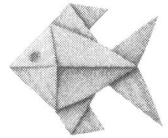

Chapter Two

I didn't see Harold at lunch but I did spot Joey eating alone at a nearby table. When he saw me looking at him, he jutted out his chin and narrowed his eyes. The look clearly said, "I hate you."

When I continued to watch him out of the corner of my eye, his jerky movements and nervous leg bouncing made me think he was hiding something.

Laura, my lunch mate and new friend, followed my line of sight and whispered across the table. "Why is that guy giving you the evil eye?"

"It's a long story," I whispered back.

"What did you say?"

Even with hearing aids, Laura didn't hear well. "I'll tell you later."

Laura and I slowly walked arm in arm out of the dining room and toward the elevator. Laura's brain was in better shape than mine, but her body was weak and she walked with pain and effort. We were quite a pair.

Since we were snail-walking and I knew Laura would get us back to our apartments, I took the opportunity to look around. Several new people had recently moved into Martyn Manor, and I nodded at them as we passed.

I was an official ambassador for the place and I stayed fairly up to date on new move-ins, so when a younger man I'd not seen before briskly walked by, my Spidey sense kicked in. I made a mental note to ask Sophia, the Manor's volunteer coordinator, about the guy. She kept a roster of newcomers.

After I returned to my apartment, I spoke briefly with Sophia over the phone. From my description, she didn't have a name for the man in the hall so I turned my attention back to Joey and his possible key-making project.

I fired up my MacBook Air and Googled *key making and duplicating*. The most interesting information I found about duplication was the following instructions: *Heat up your original key with a lighter, then press it onto a piece of clear tape. Transfer the tape onto an expired credit card, then cut out the shape of the key with scissors.*

I texted Harold my findings and he texted back.

> But he'd have to have a key to duplicate and I haven't seen him taping anything to an old credit card.

Maybe the police missed one of his skeleton keys. It wouldn't be hard to hide a key. Maybe he put it down his pants.

Harold tagged my text with a *haha* emoji, but I wasn't joking.

—

At dinner, I didn't bring up the topic of Joey because I was afraid Harold would cut me off at the pass. I knew that if I didn't press the issue, he'd be more inclined to talk to him. I did, however, ask if he'd seen a new guy around.

"What new guy?" he asked.

"That's exactly what Sophia said when I asked her," I replied while I struggled to cut my stringy roast beef.

"You asked the volunteer coordinator about this mystery man?"

I looked up at Harold. He was tipping his head to the side in the way he does when he's questioning my motives. He's always suspicious when it comes to me inquiring about things that aren't my concern. "I did. Don't you find it odd that there's a man wandering around here who no one seems to know?"

"Not particularly. He could be someone's son or nephew. He could be anybody!"

Harold sounded exasperated, but I wasn't ready to drop the subject. I swirled my lumpy mashed potatoes with my fork. "Not just anybody gets into this place. You know that. Besides, he looked creepy."

Harold took a big gulp of his burgundy. Martyn Manor recently started serving wine with dinner, so Harold no longer brought his wine to my apartment in a brown paper bag. "Creepy how?" he asked.

I knew he was indulging me, but I guessed he was also curious about an unknown man in his domain. When only twenty percent of the population is male, men tend to know one another.

"He was young, probably in his seventies." I pointed to a spot just below my ears. "He had straggly gray hair about so long and a salt and pepper beard. Not one of those cool-guy beards but a too-lazy-to-shave kind of beard. He was wearing baggy old-man jeans, a blue plaid flannel shirt, and well-worn work boots."

The Colonel looked impressed. "Wow, that was some observation you made."

"Laura walks really, really slow," I offered by way of explanation. "We saw him rushing down the hall on our way back from lunch."

"I see. And what's your intuition telling you about this stranger in our midst?"

Before answering Harold's question, I ordered the lemon meringue pie when the server came to our table. Harold ordered cherry pie with ice cream. "My intuition is telling me that he doesn't belong here. And…" I looked at Harold and wondered if I should say what was next on my mind.

"And?" he prompted.

"And, I think he has something to do with Joey."

"Joey?" Harold said in a loud voice.

I put my finger to my lips. "Shush. You want this whole place to go on high alert?" I looked around. For once, everyone seemed to be minding their own business. "Yes, Joey. I think our mystery man is somehow connected to our in-house criminal," I whispered, thankful that Harold still had reasonably good hearing.

"Let's finish this conversation in your apartment. Are you done eating?"

"Now, who's being impatient?" I took another bite. The lemon filling was just right, not too sour and not too sweet. "I'm still working on my pie. You know lemon meringue is my favorite." I stabbed another forkful and slowly put it in my mouth.

Harold smiled. "You do love your pie."

When we returned to my apartment, I sat on the love seat and Harold took the recliner. "So, what makes you think this mysterious man has something to do with Joey?" Harold asked after he pulled the lever on the chair to stick out his legs.

"Since Joey's from Brooklyn, it wouldn't be difficult for someone from his old neighborhood to show up here. Maybe Joey was in some kind of gang or associated with a ring of burglars, and this guy wants him to do another job."

Harold's knitted brow telegraphed that he was dubious about my observation. "What kind of a job?"

I kicked off my shoes and pulled the sofa blanket over my shoulders. January nights were cold in Poughkeepsie. "Making a key seems the most obvious. Let's say Mystery Man steals one of those no-copy keys, has Joey use his expertise to make a copy, returns the original after wiping off all the fingerprints, of course, then uses the new key to illegally enter a home or office. If there's no breaking and entering, the perpetrator could gradually steal money or jewels or whatever with no one being the wiser."

"That's a reach…even for you," Harold said as he took a handkerchief from his pocket and wiped his tearing eyes. He had a dry eye issue similar to mine.

We chatted a while about other things then I got up from the couch, giving Harold the clue it was time to go. He released the footrest on the recliner as I walked to the door. "Just talk to Joey, will you? Be curious about what he's doing and ask him if he's met the new guy with the beard. See how he reacts."

Harold came up beside me. "All right, Martha. I'll play along but if something serious turns up, we're calling the police sooner than later."

I gave him a salute. "Yes sir, Colonel."

Harold frowned, then he hugged me and walked out the door. My guess was he had some thinking to do. Unlike me, he didn't go about things half cocked.

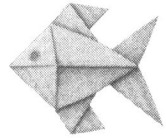

Chapter Three

I woke up the next morning feeling cranky and tired. Cold nights and sunless days didn't agree with me. As I dressed for breakfast, I wondered what my life would be like if my son had moved me to Florida instead of New York. That thought left me considering all I would have missed at Martyn Manor, most especially the friendships and escapades of the last few years.

After breakfast, I went to the exercise room and had a vigorous workout followed by a hot shower. A couple of hours later, dressed in my 80s-style sweatsuit, I made my way to Laura's apartment.

We were walking slowly to lunch when I spotted Mystery Man. I asked my friend to go ahead and find us a table. "I'll be right there," I assured her. She narrowed her eyes at me.

I boldly walked into the middle of the hallway to intercept my prey who once again seemed to be in a hurry. He stopped to avoid running me over. "Excuse me," I said in my most friendly voice. I looked up at him to make sure he was listening. "I'm an ambassador for Martyn Manor.

It's my job to meet new move-ins and I don't believe we've met." I stuck out my hand. "I'm Martha Anderson, and you are?"

The man turned his head from side to side as if he were looking for someone to rescue him. In a loud, gruff voice he said, "I'm in a hurry, lady. Get outta my way."

I stood my ground and spoke with confidence I didn't feel. "I assure you that telling me your name and shaking my hand will only take a few seconds." I gave him a fake smile.

He glared down at me. "I'm Ralph Jensen. Now move aside," he said without shaking my hand. When he stepped forward and entered my personal space, I had no recourse but to shift to the right so he could pass. He was a big guy, probably close to 300 pounds, at least six foot two with beefy arms. His cheeks were flushed above his beard, and his skin was lined and dotted with brown spots, which were probably caused by too much sun. He looked like a guy who'd spent a lot of time working outside.

I saw Laura seated at a table waiting for her lunch tray to be delivered, so I filled my tray with a Cobb salad and iced tea, then joined her.

"So?"

For an author, Laura could be a woman of few words.

"His name is Ralph Jensen, and he's not at all friendly."

"Anything else?" she prompted.

"He's aggressive and I think he's had a career in construction or something else that requires working in the sun," I said, summarizing my encounter.

"Or," Laura smiled mischievously then whispered, "he's spent time burying bodies and selling crack on the corner."

My heart did a little happy dance. It seemed as though I'd found my new partner in crime detection. "Exactly!"

"I haven't always written books about exotic places. I've also written a few mysteries and…what was the guy's name again?"

"Ralph."

"Oh yes, Ralph sounds like a character in a murder mystery to me. What do you think?" Laura demurely sipped her iced tea as if she were just another sweet old lady living incognito at Martyn Manor.

I leaned in so Laura could hear me speaking low. "I think he's somehow involved with Joey Russo."

"Who?" Laura asked.

I opened my mouth slightly. "You don't know about Joey?" I asked, amazed that she hadn't heard stories about our infamous resident.

"I'm new here, remember?"

Laura and I had recently met in my capacity as Ambassador. I'd joined the team to greet recent move-ins, hoping to make new friends. So far, Laura was the only friend I'd made but she was a gem.

"After lunch, we'll go back to my place and I'll enlighten you." I sat back and concentrated on eating my salad.

"I love a good story," Laura mused. A smile lit up her wrinkled face before she dove into a steaming bowl of vegetable beef soup.

—

I could easily imagine that in her younger days, Laura was what my dad would call, "a looker." She still had deep blue, inquisitive eyes, nicely shaped eyebrows, and high cheekbones. Her thin, white, curly hair softened her features. She reminded me of an older version of my beloved Missy who died last year alone (her choice, not mine) in the skilled care section of Martyn Manor. We'd been more than just friends and I teared up just thinking of her.

Earlier in my so-called PI career, Missy, along with my friend, Madge, were my crime-solving partners. Madge later returned to Canada to enter a treatment program for alcohol addiction.

For me, one of the most difficult aspects of growing old was losing friends. All of my original Martyn Manor friends were gone, with the exception of Harold and Molly, who might as well be gone since she'd become involved in an all-consuming relationship with Rodney, her boyfriend.

When Laura circled her finger as a sign to speed it up, I shut down my reverie of lost friends and finished my salad.

—

At Martyn Manor, it's considered a rite of passage when you're invited into a friend's apartment. So, even though Laura and I had been having lunch together for a few months, this was the first time she'd been in my personal space. I had visited her apartment early on when I went there to pick up a book she'd offered to loan me. At the time, I felt like I'd time-traveled back to the 1950s.

After I unlocked and opened the door, Laura entered my apartment and looked around. "Very modern. A total reflection of you, Martha."

I offered her the navy blue, leather recliner. "I'll take that as a compliment," I said as I made myself comfortable on the love seat. "I came to live here rather suddenly. My son whisked me away from my home in Iowa, gave away most of my belongings, and settled me in here," I waved my arm around, "furniture and all. Fortunately, his wife, now ex-wife, has very good taste."

Laura flipped her hand in the air as if dismissing the surroundings. I could tell from her apartment that she considered up-to-date creature comforts inconsequential.

"So, tell me about this Joey character," she said in her investigative-author voice.

"Remember the guy sitting alone at the table across from us at lunch recently?" I began, not sure Laura would remember.

"The guy who gave you a dirty look?"

"Yes, that's the one."

Before I could continue, Laura asked, "What was that all about?"

I liked Laura's enthusiasm, but I needed to speak uninterrupted if I was to remember the details of the story. "I'll get to all that, just be patient."

"Sorry."

I told Laura about the false fire alarms and an illegal entry to my apartment that happened two years ago.

"Joey did that? Did you catch him?"

"We sure did!" I exclaimed with some pride.

"Tell me more."

I settled back into the cushions and felt a small smile creep across my lips as I recalled the setup. "I had a minicam in my apartment because someone had stolen my credit card numbers and I was trying to catch them in the act. By the way, Joey wasn't that person."

"Who was? Did you catch him?"

"It was a her and yes, I did."

Laura leaned forward in her chair, apparently intrigued. "And…"

"The former assisted living director, Agnes Duly, was caught on camera stealing my credit card numbers. She was arrested and fired. Believe me, we were all happy to see her go. She wasn't a nice lady."

"Good grief! That was quite a catch!" exclaimed Laura.

"It was. Now, getting back to the Joey story…" I leaned forward on the couch while I dredged up the memory. "After I'd captured a video of him entering my apartment, I put two and two together and figured that if he could open my locked door, he could probably open a locked fire alarm case. I called the fire department, who sent someone out to dust the alarm cases for fingerprints and they later confirmed that the perpetrator was Joey." I sat back, tired from all the remembering.

"Don't stop now, Martha. Tell me why he's still living here."

I took a deep breath. "He told my friend Harold that he was fined a thousand dollars for setting off the alarms and was under house arrest for illegally entering my apartment. He reports monthly to a probation officer, but that's it. I think he's still up to no good and this Ralph-guy is somehow involved."

Laura scooted to the edge of her chair. "Seems to me that Joey got off easy. Probably because he's old."

"Exactly!"

"And I thought this place was boring," Laura said under her breath.

I simply shook my head, too tired to say more.

"I can see that this storytelling and remembering the past has you all wrung out." Laura slowly got up from the recliner, her knees cracking. "Go take a nap. You look done in."

I eased myself to the edge of the couch to walk Laura to the door but she motioned for me to stay seated. "Don't get up. I'll see myself out."

I leaned back into the cushions. "I'll pick you up for lunch tomorrow. Good talking to you." I gave her a little wave. "Bye."

Since I wasn't a fan of naps, I left the couch, took the laptop from my dinette table, then moved to the recliner to get comfortable. After sitting back with my eyes closed for a few minutes, I entered my password and asked Mr. Google to look up Joey Russo, Brooklyn, New York.

I was wondering why I hadn't thought of doing this earlier when Joey's photo popped up on my screen. It was a younger version of him, but there was no doubt it was Joey. Below his picture was a newspaper article about him being arrested as a suspect in a bank robbery. I scrolled down the page. I couldn't find any information on him serving time, but the fact he was arrested, was probably why his fingerprints had been in the system when the fire marshal checked the database before he was accused of setting off fire alarms in the building.

The possibility of him being part of a bank heist led me to believe he might have salted away money from the robbery to use for his retirement years which, as it had turned out, were here at Martyn Manor. This place wasn't cheap, so Joey had to have a bundle.

Thankfully, my son Richard paid my bill. My two daughters also contributed, but he was the one to move me halfway across the country to this particular assisted living facility because it was near his home. He'd paid my entrance fee and started the monthly payments two and a half years ago when he decided I could no longer safely live alone. The incident that set off his alarm bells was when I'd left the stove on, which caused a pot to burn and the fire department to be dispatched. It wasn't my first indiscretion, but it was the most serious.

I brought my attention back to the computer screen and made a note to tell Laura about my findings at lunch tomorrow. I must have dozed off because I awoke with a start and realized it was nearly time to get dressed for dinner. Maybe Harold could shed some light on the situation.

—

Harold didn't bring up Joey at dinner so neither did I. My information about Joey's possible past involvement in a bank robbery could wait. I looked around the dining room. Not seeing Joey or Ralph, I wondered about their whereabouts. Perhaps they went out to eat, or maybe Ralph had already vacated the premises.

That evening, after listening to our own lovely Charmaine play oldies but goodies on the piano, I returned to my apartment and put on my cozy burgundy robe and nightgown. Although I was tired, my mind was churning.

Were Ralph and Joey planning another heist? It didn't seem like Ralph was here for a neighborly visit. Why had he been so hostile to me? Did Joey tell him that I was responsible for his arrest? This seemed unlikely. What tough guy from Brooklyn wanted to admit he got made by a little old lady? Was there another mystery brewing at Martyn Manor? After drinking a nice cup of chamomile tea, I eventually went to bed and fell asleep.

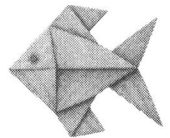

Chapter Four

I was suddenly awakened by howling wind and something else, a tiny swath of light and a swish. I stayed perfectly still, listening with every fiber of my being. Then, after about a minute, I heard the click of my door latch.

I sat up, wondering if my imagination was playing tricks on me or had someone been in my apartment. With my heart pounding, I leaned back on my pillow to get a grip on my emotions.

My need to go to the bathroom finally drove me out from under the warm covers. "Alexa, what time is it?"

She responded. "It's 2:21 am."

I tried to imagine Alexa as a floppy-eared golden retriever lying beside my bed. After I returned from the bathroom, I was wide awake so I struggled into my robe, shuffled to the living room, and turned on a light.

My first instinct was to check the door. It was unlocked! Positive that I had locked it before going to bed, I again pushed in the button, then made a mental note to ask maintenance to install a bolt lock ASAP.

I walked across the room to my mini fridge. Since I no longer had staff visitations in the evening, I only stocked a few cans of soda. When I opened the door, the soft light from the fridge interior looked familiar, and my heart sped up as I remembered the light I'd seen from my bed.

There were three cans on the shelf, just as there were the last time I'd checked. However, when I bent down to scrutinize the sodas more closely, I realized that one can was full-sized. I always bought minis.

Had Joey broken into my apartment and, once again, stolen a can of soda, then left another in its place? Was it meant to be a warning or was he simply proving to himself that he still had the balls to do it?

I considered calling someone, but who would I call and what would I tell them? On second thought, if it was Joey and he left fingerprints, maybe they'd remove him from the Manor and put him in a cushy, low-security prison where he belonged.

I finally wore myself out thinking about the what-ifs and decided to sort the whole thing out in the light of day. The wind was still roaring, throwing pellets of icy snow against my window. I shivered at the thought of a February blizzard raging outside and a creepy old man sneaking into my apartment in the middle of the night.

When I looked out my bedroom window, the streetlights were out and it was as dark as a black cat in a hole. Thankfully, the Manor had a backup generator.

"Alexa, play soft music for five minutes." I climbed into bed and drew up the covers. Music filled the room, and I was comforted by the sound and the knowledge that I was still connected to the outside world.

—

The following morning, my memory of a possible intruder was fuzzy. Had I seen a flash of light coming from the fridge, or did it come from the storm raging outside? Was my hearing still good enough to recognize the sound of my door clicking shut?

At lunch, I told Laura about my Internet findings concerning Joey, but for some reason, I left out my possible intruder experience. I had, however, called maintenance first thing and asked them to install a bolt lock.

"You didn't tell me Joey was from Brooklyn," Laura said. "My grandson is a precinct captain there. I bet he'd get us the scoop on this guy's past if he has an arrest record."

"You do? He would?" My adrenaline started flowing just thinking about the possibilities.

Laura gave me a wry smile. "Don't get too excited, my friend. This may lead to a dead-end, but being on your team makes my life more interesting, so I'll call Donny, that's my grandson, and ask him about Joey Russo. It might take a while for him to get back to me."

I took a sip of my iced tea. Even though the weather outside was cold and blustery, I still liked drinking iced tea at lunch. "I'll wait patiently."

Laura cocked her head as if she doubted the truth of my response.

To show her I could be patient, I said, "I'm waiting patiently for Harold to talk to Joey and find out what he's up to in the woodworking shop. It seems suspicious that he's using tin snips on metal."

Laura's brows came together. "Why?"

"Keys. Joey was an expert with locks and keys. Remember?"

"Oh, yes." She leaned in like she was eager for more information.

I rested my elbows on the table. "Harold thinks I need to mind my own business."

Laura dabbed at her lips with her napkin. Once again, her mannerisms reminded me of Missy. "Can't you entice him to be part of our team?"

I smiled at the 'our team' reference. "I don't know." I considered how Laura had just offered to get info on Joey. "Maybe if I tell Harold about you asking your grandson to help us he'll come around. He won't want to be left behind and have some young whippersnapper be the hero."

"Men," Laura said.

Her statement didn't need a reply. I understood the sentiment.

When I returned from lunch, the new bolt lock was in place. I congratulated myself on acting responsibly. I also wondered what I'd tell Harold when he noticed the new lock. He didn't miss a thing.

—

Just as I suspected, when Harold picked me up for dinner, he pointed at the door. "What's this?"

"A new lock."

"How come?"

"I may have had an intruder last night, so I asked maintenance for an extra lock."

Harold put his hands on his hips. "An intruder! And you're just now getting around to mentioning this?"

"I didn't actually see anyone. I heard noises during the storm and saw a flash of light that I thought might have come from the mini fridge. A can of soda may be missing, and a new one was possibly added." When Harold didn't respond, I said, "My memory of the incident is fuzzy. Maybe it was all my imagination."

"Did you tell anyone?"

"What would I say? The police would think I was a daft old lady, which I am, and dismiss it out of hand. If I told anyone in authority around here, they'd think I was reliving my glory days when I actually had proof of Joey entering my apartment. Besides, maybe it wasn't even Joey. Maybe it was simply my imagination."

"You have a point. You want me to stay the night just in case someone comes in again?" He gave me a shy grin.

I pointed to the new lock. "I think that will take care of future intruders." I looked up at Harold. "Don't you?"

"Probably. As long as you remember to use it. After I leave, I'll wait to hear the bolt slide before I start walking down the hall."

I nodded. "Not necessary, but I know you're going to do it anyway."

"Yep. Good night. Sleep tight."

After Harold walked out, I pushed the button on the lock, then slid the new bolt into place. I heard his footsteps moving slowly down the hall.

Chapter Five

I had a peaceful night's sleep knowing I was safely locked inside my apartment. Unfortunately, the peace was short-lived.

When I returned to my apartment after lunch, I found a note taped to my door. This wasn't a sweet sentiment like I'd found when I was in my "relationship phase" a couple of years ago. This one was threatening. Written in all caps with a black marker, the words were, MIND YOUR OWN DAMN BUSINESS!!

Butterflies filled my stomach, and I was reminded that Joey and his cohorts weren't good guys. I wondered if my life was in danger. Did Joey leave the note or was it from Ralph? Had Joey been in my apartment last night and this was the follow-up? The stormy, middle-of-the-night experience was starting to fade from my memory like a dream.

I threw the note in a drawer in case I needed it for evidence someday, then I pushed the threat to the back of my mind. I refused to be bullied.

When we returned to my apartment after dinner, I decided not to tell Harold about the nasty note. He was probably still digesting the intruder story. If I showed him the note, I knew he'd want me to notify the police, and I wasn't ready to do that. I did, however, tell him about Laura's grandson's possible involvement. He suddenly came forth with information, just like I'd predicted.

"I still don't know what Joey is making out of metal, but I do know he has an ex-wife living nearby. Apparently, there's bad blood between them." I settled down in the recliner. "Well, that's an interesting tidbit. How did you happen to get that out of him?" Harold's cheeks were pinkening up. I could tell he was getting hooked. He'd soon come around and be a team player just like he'd been in the past.

"I didn't have to 'get it out of him.' He started the conversation by asking me how I could possibly associate with you." Harold chuckled.

I wasn't amused. "And…" I left a pregnant pause. When he didn't say more, I prompted, "What did you tell him?"

"Coming up with a response was tricky. Knowing that Joey has a lot of animosity toward you, I didn't want to sound like we were as close as we are, so I simply said you were someone to eat dinner with and left it at that."

Harold gave me a serious look. "You know he blames you for the trouble he got himself into. To him, setting off fire alarms and stealing a can of soda was just being Joey."

"By the way…" I decided now was the ideal time to bring up what I'd discovered on the Internet, and I told

Harold about Joey's possible involvement with a bank heist. "It makes me think he's a hardened criminal." To my disappointment, Harold didn't seem surprised by my new intel.

"Possibly," Harold paused, then continued, "and if he knew you and Laura were investigating his past, I think he'd be furious. You're treading on thin ice here, Martha. The guy could be dangerous." Harold looked over at me. "Be especially careful about what you say in the dining room. There are a lot of big ears in there. You wouldn't want anything to get back to Joey." He gave me another look. "Do you understand me?"

I saluted. Harold hates it when I do that, but I'm not fond of his advice-giving even when I know it's for my own good. "Yes, sir."

Harold frowned.

I redirected the conversation. "Did he tell you his ex-wife's name?"

"Rose or Rosa, something like that. He warned me about women and how they can mess up a guy's life. Hell, I'm 93 years old! I'm not some 16-year-old kid who has no idea about how to handle relationships. His remarks were insulting, but I played along so he'd think he could trust me."

Harold was definitely coming around. I got up from the recliner, walked across the room, then sat down at the table where my computer was charging. "Let's look up Rosa."

Harold joined me at the table and watched as I plugged *Rosa Russo* into the search engine. There wasn't much there other than her address in Poughkeepsie and the fact that she was retired from City Insurance Agency in Brooklyn. The TruthFinder website probably had more detailed information but I wasn't willing to pay a fee to get it. Not yet, anyway.

"Brooklyn definitely ties this Rosa to Joey, don't you think?" I asked Harold.

"Probably."

"They must have divorced after they moved to Poughkeepsie. Maybe she got the house and he got Martyn Manor." I looked up at Harold. "Why's he here anyway? For an old guy, he seems healthy enough."

"I asked him that once. He said he has a condition called syncope and diabetes."

I closed my laptop and gave Harold my full attention. "Never heard of syncope. Did he elaborate?"

"Yes. I was getting to that."

Harold doesn't like it when I'm impatient. I can't blame him.

"He said that syncope is a temporary loss of consciousness caused by a sudden fall in blood pressure. He told me that after he'd passed out a few times in his condo, he realized he couldn't live alone. Apparently, the staff here checks on him several times a day to make sure he's okay," Harold explained.

"Good grief! No wonder he never seems to leave this place."

"Well, that and he's under house arrest," Harold reminded me.

"Oh yeah." I changed the subject to the Mastery Man, who was now known as Ralph. "Did you ask him if he knew Ralph?"

"Who's Ralph?"

I'd forgotten that I hadn't filled Harold in about my encounter. "That's Mystery Man's name."

Harold narrowed his eyes. "And you know this because…"

I explained how I'd approached the guy in my capacity as official ambassador and introduced myself. I didn't include the part about blocking his forward momentum in the hall, but I could tell I wasn't fooling Harold.

"And he just nicely shook your hand and volunteered his name?"

I grimaced. "Well, not exactly. He wasn't a particularly friendly sort of guy."

Harold let out a sigh of exasperation. "So now you've managed to make an enemy of not one but two scary and questionable men."

"Not exactly an enemy…." I trailed off. "I'll stay away from Ralph if you'll continue to chat with Joey," I bargained.

"He's not exactly someone I enjoy chatting with, but I'll see what I can do." Harold got up from his chair, came up behind me, and put his cheek on the top of my head. "Only for you, Martha. Only for you."

He walked to the door. "Be sure and lock up after I leave. Good night. See you tomorrow."

I walked over to Harold and gave him a little kiss. "Good night. Thanks for joining the team." He shook his head before firmly closing the door behind him. After I slid the bolt lock in place, I heard him step away from the door.

Chapter Six

The February blizzard was followed by a succession of cold and snowy days that kept me from my weekly trip to the library. I missed getting out, but I also knew that walking on icy, snow-packed sidewalks was risky for an old lady like me. However, the bad weather didn't keep my son from his monthly lunch visit.

"You're looking well, Mother," Richard said after settling himself at a table in the dining room.

Richard was my firstborn and only son. He was also a retired attorney and divorced.

"Thank you. I'm feeling quite chipper but I'm getting cabin fever. How were the roads today?"

"The roads are good but the sidewalks are still slippery. You're wise to stay inside for now." My son is always extra cautious so his evaluation might or might not have been completely accurate.

"What's new with you?" I asked to keep the conversation going. Richard wasn't good at chit-chat.

Richard stirred his bean soup. While still looking into his bowl, he said, "I've met someone."

"Would you like to elaborate?"

Richard's cheeks grew pink. "We met on OurTime, an Internet dating site for singles over fifty."

"Well, you're definitely over fifty." Richard was sixty-six.

He gave me a tiny smile. "Fifty to seventy felt like a good range."

"No judgment here, tell me more." I leaned in. I didn't have to fake my interest. I really did wonder who my son had attracted into his life. He was handsome and successful but his people skills weren't great.

"Her name is Gloria, she's retired from human resources, divorced, and has an adult daughter. She lives in a condo here in Poughkeepsie. She possesses season tickets to the Hudson Valley Symphony Orchestra and we've attended twice." Richard sat back with a look of satisfaction on his face for having given me, what he considered, a thorough description of his new lady friend.

"I didn't know you were an aficionado of the symphony," I ventured.

"When the experience comes with an attractive woman, I can learn to be."

What a bold statement for my son to make! Could this woman be transforming him into someone who was more open and responsive? "When can I meet her?"

"Let's see how the next few weeks go. If all goes well, perhaps I'll bring her to lunch next month."

"I'd like that." I wanted to support my son in this new relationship. Although I rather liked living alone, I knew it wasn't a picnic for a single man his age.

"Speaking of relationships, how's Harold?" Richard asked.

Richard knew Harold from a court visit a few years ago, and Harold was my 'plus one' at Richard's daughter's wedding. They'd also met from time to time at the Manor. "Harold's good. Thanks for asking. He picks me up and we have dinner together every night. We always find something to talk about and he's good company."

"I'm happy for you. I guess moving you to Martyn Manor turned out to be a good decision after all."

I nodded. I never resented being moved, even though it was abrupt. "You've been very generous, Richard, and I appreciate having such a lovely place to spend my last days."

"Days?" Richard echoed with alarm.

"I'm over ninety. I don't look too far ahead."

Richard laid his napkin aside, the sign that it was time for him to go.

I popped the last bite of my chicken wrap into my mouth. "I'll look forward to possibly meeting Gloria next month."

"We'll see. Stay well, Mother."

—

The first week of March was sunny with warmer temperatures, so by Wednesday, I deemed it safe to travel to the library in the Manor's minivan. Breathing in the cool air was literally and figuratively a breath of fresh air after being cooped up for nearly a month.

During the bumpy ride with the inside of the minivan smelling faintly of gasoline, I thought about Winter, the young librarian who frequently helped me find books. I was fascinated by her outrageous pink, nearly shaved head, her multiple piercings, and tattoos. In fact, since I swam in a sea of white-haired old ladies, Winter was one reason I enjoyed visiting the library. She hadn't been at the desk for the last couple of months and I hoped she'd returned.

The sidewalk to the library's entrance was clear, so I briskly walked to the door, went inside, returned my books, and approached the desk, happy to see that Winter was back on duty. She greeted me and asked about my health. I told her I was fine, then asked if she could recommend a good mystery. I was done with romance novels; they were so last year.

"I have just what you're looking for." When Winter stepped out from behind the counter, I was surprised to see that she was pregnant. Not maybe-she-gained-a- little-weight but definitely pregnant. I hoped she'd shed some light on the subject while we walked to the stacks.

Winter's extended belly didn't slow her down and I hurried along beside her. When she wasn't forthcoming with information, I asked the obvious question. "When's your baby due?"

"Oh, she's not my baby. I'm a surrogate for a couple from a neighboring town."

My mouth must have dropped open because Winter added, "You know, I'm having this baby for them. The husband donated his sperm."

"I'm aware of what surrogacy means. That's very, ahh, very generous of you."

Winter looked as though she could deliver any minute. Rather than the loose-fitting clothes we wore in my day, today's pregnant women seem to prefer tight-fitting clothing that shows off their baby bumps. Winter wore a long, green knit dress. She looked like she'd swallowed a pumpkin. For the first time, I noticed tiny heart-shaped tattoos running down her neck from her earlobe and a lovely green stone hanging from on a cord around her neck. I was about to comment on the stone when she continued.

"I'm due early May and the parents are actually the ones who are being generous. They're paying me enough that I can go back to school and get my degree. I'll be off from work for a few weeks but then I'll be back. I'm going to attend classes in the afternoon and work here in the morning, so I'll still see you." She looked at me. "Unless you change your schedule."

My goodness. That was more than Winter had said to me since we'd met the year I was looking for romantic novels during that particular interlude of my life. Perhaps pregnancy agreed with her. I couldn't imagine giving up a baby I'd carried for nine months, but each to their own.

We'd reached the stacks where the preferred mysteries were located. "Good luck with everything, Winter." When she didn't respond, I added, "Your necklace is lovely, by the way."

Winter fingered the smooth green stone. "It's my totem." Then she pulled out a book and handed it to me. Maybe she hadn't changed so much after all. "I recommend you start with a cozy mystery."

"Cozy?"

"Cozy mysteries have only mild profanity, murders without the blood or violence, and intrigue. The main character is frequently a woman who sees herself as an amateur sleuth."

I wondered how I'd missed knowing about this genre. A cozy mystery was exactly what I was looking for. "Thanks."

With that, Winter was on her way back to the desk. She had an obvious waddle and something else I hadn't noticed before. A slight limp.

Winter's recommendation was *The Thursday Murder Club* by Richard Osman. I turned the book over and read the description. Satisfied that it was right up my alley, I put the book in my bag and wondered if I'd ever be part of a murder investigation again.

I thought that witnessing someone being murdered on a cruise ship was more than enough excitement, but I'd recently grown restless. Maybe experiencing a murder mystery in a book would satisfy my itch for investigating and solving real crimes.

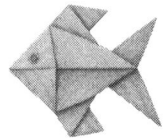

Chapter Seven

I exited the minivan, walked through the front door, and ran smack-dab into my arch nemesis, Ethyl Haggerty.

"Where have you been?" she asked as if it were a crime to leave the premises.

I wanted to say that it was none of her damn business, but instead, I said, "I've been to the library." I held up my book bag to show her the evidence, then I started walking toward the elevator. She followed me.

"I saw you speaking with that young man last week. Is he a relative of yours?"

"What young man are you talking about?" I asked. I wasn't going to make this interrogation easy.

"The one with the long hair and beard."

"No, he's not a relative. In fact, I was wondering why he's been nosing around here. I'm surprised you don't know all about him."

Ethyl got into the elevator with me. "Well, I don't." Ethyl stabbed at the button for our floor.

When I first moved to the Manor, Ethyl snitched on me and I'd gotten into trouble. I hated to befriend her, but desperate times called for desperate measures. I appealed to her ego. "I'm sure you'll know all about him soon enough. When you do, will you let me in on your findings? He must have a relative or some connection to this place or they wouldn't have allowed him in."

We exited the elevator. Ethyl went right and I turned left. I was glad that it was still early enough in the day that I wasn't directionally challenged.

"Maybe," Ethyl said as we parted ways.

I returned to my apartment and started reading my new library book about a group of oldsters who gathered to solve cold cases and later became involved with a murder. It gave me the itch to find out who Ralph was, what Joey Russo was up to, and who had entered my apartment in the middle of the night.

—

Mid-month, Richard informed me he'd be coming to lunch on Friday and bringing Gloria. I added her name to my guest list.

My son and his new girlfriend had already gone through the cafeteria line when I joined them at the table with my bowl of tomato soup and grilled cheese sandwich. I needed comfort food today.

Richard's ex-wife, Maria, was of Spanish descent and beautiful. Gloria was also very attractive with similar coloring. I guessed she was Italian with dark hair and eyes. She wasn't as tall as Maria, but she had a nice figure. She wore a skirt that sat well above her knees and a tight blue sweater. Her boobs were normal size, but she managed to show more cleavage than seemed appropriate. On first impression, Gloria also seemed to be the polar opposite of my staid, risk-adverse, buttoned-up, lawyer son.

Gloria reached out and hugged me. "I'm so happy to meet you, Mrs. Anderson."

"It's also nice meeting you, Gloria. Please call me Martha," I said as I quickly disengaged. I was much more "out there" than my son, but I wasn't particularly fond of hugging complete strangers.

"How long have you lived in Poughkeepsie?" I asked.

"I moved into my condo last year," Gloria replied.

"I hear you enjoy the symphony?" Now that I'd met her, I certainly wouldn't have pegged Gloria as a symphony-goer.

"Yes, it's nice to live where season tickets don't cost an arm and a leg." She smiled at my son. "Besides the symphony, Richard has taken me to Mahoney's Irish Pub and Steakhouse. He said your 90th birthday party was held there."

Mahoney's seemed to be more Gloria's style. It had karaoke during the week and the place held special memories for me from earlier days. If Gloria and Richard only knew!

I pulled myself back to the present and asked, "Did you do karaoke when you were there?"

"We went on a quiet night but karaoke sounds like fun. Let's the three of us go sometime," Gloria suggested with enthusiasm.

Richard turned slightly pale but didn't respond. I stayed quiet, figuring that it was up to the two of them to work this out.

We chatted for a few minutes. Then, out of the blue, Gloria asked. "You happen to know Joey Russo? I heard he lives here."

I nearly choked on my tea. All I could do was nod my head up and down, which was enough for Gloria to ramble on.

"My neighbor, Rosa, is this Russo guy's ex-wife. She talks about him all the time. They're both from my old neighborhood." Gloria loaded her fork with salad and waved it about. "She's always bad-mouthing him. Seems he owes her a lot of money. I just thought that since there don't seem to be many men in this place…" Gloria looked around to confirm her intel, "that you mighta heard of him." She finally popped the salad into her mouth.

"I've heard of him. Tell me more about Rosa. Her story sounds interesting, and I'm always up for a good story." I gave Gloria an innocent smile of encouragement, then returned to my soup. I certainly didn't want to reveal my past concerning Joey, not with my son sitting across the table.

Gloria fidgeted with her lettuce, then took another bite. Although she seemed nervous, she also showed signs of being delighted to have engaged the attention of her boyfriend's mother.

"Well, it seems that Joey used to run with a group of gangsta-types. Not drug dealers or anything like that, more along the lines of petty thieves. But" Gloria leaned in conspiratorially, "according to Rosa, they did do a big bank heist back in the day and got away with it." She straightened up. "Eventually, Joey and Rosa moved here to Poughkeepsie to get away from the heat…" Gloria paused briefly then leaned in. "If you know what I mean."

She didn't seem to notice Richard's wide-eyed look. Apparently he was seeing a side of Gloria that he hadn't seen before. Brooklyn Gal was the flip side of Symphony Lady.

"I don't blame her for being pissed," Gloria continued. "All Rosa got out of the divorce was a two-bedroom condo. No spousal support. They'd owned a house together but had to sell it when Joey moved in here. He told her he had fainting spells, but she doesn't buy it."

I couldn't help myself, I just had to ask about Mystery Man. "Has Rosa ever mentioned someone named Ralph Jensen?" I asked Gloria.

She looked thoughtful for a minute. "I don't think so. Why?"

"I just wondered because I think he might be a friend of Joey's."

Gloria looked delighted. "So, you KNOW Joey!"

"Not well. My friend Harold frequently sees him in the woodworking shop. That's about it." It was another white lie, but even Richard didn't know about me getting Joey arrested. I hoped Rosa didn't know about it either. If Rosa passed the story to Gloria, and she passed it to Richard, there would be A LOT of questions.

"Rosa said Joey got into some kind of trouble here about a year or so ago. I thought you might've heard something about that."

I drew my brows together as if I were trying to remember. "My memory isn't that great. Right, Richard?" I looked at my son, who had turned noticeably pale.

Richard put his napkin on the table, a signal that he was ready to leave, but Gloria wasn't the wiser.

"Well, Rich, aren't you going to answer your mother?"

"Mother's right. Her memory isn't as good as it once was. That's why she lives here," Richard squeaked out.

Gloria reached over and patted my hand. I had to admit, the woman was growing on me.

"Well, she seems perfectly fine to me," she said, addressing my son.

Letting Richard off the hook and giving him an opportunity to be on his way, I concluded the conversation. "I'd be interested in learning more about Rosa and her connection to the Manor. I don't get out much, so I always like hearing about people in the" I pointed toward the windows "outside world. I'm already looking forward to our next get-together."

Richard got up. "We don't want to tire Mother out, Gloria."

She jumped up, quickly pulling down her skirt. "Oh, of course not!" She hugged me again. "It was lovely meeting you, Martha."

"It was nice meeting you too, Gloria. Let's keep in touch."

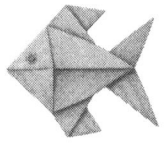

Chapter Eight

That night I hurried Harold through dinner. I couldn't wait to tell him about Gloria and what she'd said about Joey. "Let's take our desserts in to-go containers and eat them in my apartment," I suggested.

"Patience, Martha," Harold said as he ordered a chocolate sundae that wouldn't do well in a to-go box.

"But I might forget what I have to tell you," I said before ordering a chocolate eclair to-go.

"Have a decaf while I enjoy my ice cream. Knowing you, every detail that went in…" he pointed to my head, "will come right out the mouth. I'm not worried." He took a big bite of his sundae after passing me the maraschino cherry on a stem.

Harold was right. After we returned to my apartment, I was able to remember every detail of my conversation with Gloria.

Per usual, Harold listened intently. "A bank heist, huh? Well, that adds some meat to the pot."

"What kind of saying is that?"

"You have your Dadisms, I have my Haroldisms."

I tried not to seem too excited but Harold was on to me. "I see that gleam in your eyes again."

"Well, that gleam will get even brighter if you'll stir the pot and ask Joey questions like, 'Do you know Ralph Jensen? When is your ex-wife coming for a visit?' and 'What are you making with metal scraps?'"

Harold held up his hand. "Hold on. Let's take one thing at a time. Joey said he didn't know when his ex was going to visit him, but he definitely wasn't looking forward to it. Maybe he'll refuse to put her on his visitors' list."

Harold held up two fingers, indicating he was on to my next question. "He got very nervous when I questioned him about Jensen. When he asked me how I knew the guy, I told him I'd seen him around. Joey said he knew him from back in the day, but he was also an unwelcome visitor."

"And the last bit about what he's making?"

"I still have no idea. Yesterday, he was fiddling around with some wire. Too bad you don't work in the shop, then you could question him yourself," Harold added with a "humph."

"I'm the last person he'd give the time of day to. You know that. And now that I know someone who knows his ex," I paused for emphasis, "wow, I'd really be on his 'worst person in the place' list."

I took my eclair out of the box and offered some to Harold. When he declined, I took a bite, then told him about meeting up with Ethyl a few weeks ago. I'd forgotten to tell him at the time, but the conversation seemed more important now based on what we'd recently learned.

My eclair transported me back to France, my favorite place on earth, but I didn't linger there. "I bet she'll get intel on Ralph. She's like a bloodhound. Once she gets a whiff of something there's no stopping her. Plus, now she's extra motivated to get information I don't have. Coming up with something would delight her to no end. I just wish she'd get on with it."

Under his breath, Harold murmured, "Women."

I shook my finger at him. "You just wait. I bet I'll get more intel from Ethyl than you got from Joey, and he was the target of Jensen's visit."

—

Sure enough, early the next morning Ethyl caught me in the hall. Normally, she wasn't out of her apartment before nine, so I figured she'd been waiting for me to go to breakfast.

"Good morning, Ethyl. What brings you out so early?" I wanted to let her know that I was on to her shenanigans.

Walking with me to the elevator, she asked, "Have you found out anything about Ralph yet?"

"No, but I imagine you have."

Ethyl almost looked giddy. "You'd be right about that."

"Well, are you going to share or are you holding the information for ransom?"

Ethyl narrowed her eyes. "Why is intelligence on him so important to you?"

I shrugged my shoulders. "No reason. I'm just a naturally curious person."

"Yeah, right," Ethyl said.

We got on the elevator. I wondered how long she was going to hold out on me. She was enjoying this way too much. "Well?"

The elevator door opened and we walked out. "Let's have breakfast together and I'll tell you all I know," Ethyl bargained.

As much as I didn't want to have breakfast with this woman, or anyone else for that matter, the sacrifice was worth it. "All right, but this better be good," I said.

Ethyl led the way and took a seat at her usual table. She was in full control and I could tell she was savoring every minute. I tried to be patient while she stirred cream into her coffee, buttered her toast, added jam, and then slowly and carefully placed a napkin in her lap. She loudly slurped her coffee before leaning across the table.

"I can't disclose my sources," Ethyl said with great authority, "but I was told that Ralph Jensen is an ex-con from Brooklyn and an old friend of Joey Russo."

I tried to keep all expression from my face when Ethyl looked for my reaction. "Go on."

"Apparently, Jensen spent time in Cayuga Correctional Facility, a medium-security state prison. I don't know how long he was there but he went into the place in the '90s." Ethyl took a bite of her toast then licked the dripped jam off her fingers.

"What was he in for?" I asked.

"I'm getting to that," Ethyl wasn't going to be rushed. She wanted the whole place to see that she was having breakfast with Martha Anderson, and she wanted me to wait with bated breath as long as possible.

"He and his gang robbed a bodega and roughed up the clerk. Jensen was caught on tape and a year later, he was sentenced to five years. His buddies were initially suspects, but they got off because they weren't on the tape and the cops didn't believe the bodega owner when he told them they were accomplices."

When Ethyl paused, I added my two cents. "Sounds like they might have had a cop or two in their pockets."

"Maybe." Ethyl's forehead wrinkled. She didn't like being interrupted.

"You have some source! That's a lot of detail regarding Jensen." I was a bit jealous. Ethyl and her apparent contact person would make great additions to my little troop of two, but since I could barely tolerate Ethyl, including her was out of the question, so I dismissed the notion and quickly finished my breakfast.

"Thanks for sharing your information. He certainly doesn't sound like the kind of person we want wandering the halls of Martyn Manor." I got up from the table and pushed in my chair.

"Certainly not!" Ethyl resumed eating her breakfast.

—

When I talked to Laura at lunch, I learned that she hadn't gleaned much additional information about Joey from her grandson.

He confirmed that although Russo hadn't served time, his name appeared as a suspect in a bodega robbery and an unsolved bank heist several years ago. His name was also associated with Ralph Jensen and two other men who were under suspicion for illegal activity but that was the extent of his record, with the exception of a brief mention of his fine and the fact that he was currently under house arrest in Poughkeepsie.

Joey seemed to have an invisible cloak protecting him from crimes in which he'd probably been involved. Maybe he wasn't as dangerous as Harold thought. Or maybe Harold wanted to scare me away from putting my nose in where he thought it didn't belong.

Chapter Nine

The day before our monthly lunch, Richard called to cancel. He gave a lame excuse about needing to get his car serviced. He didn't mention Gloria, so I didn't inquire. Richard had never canceled a lunch, not even when the weather was terrible. I thought it was suspicious and I wondered about the real reason.

—

While I was eating breakfast the next morning, Gloria called to ask if it was all right to come to lunch without Richard.

"Of course. I'll put your name on my visitor's list and meet you in the dining room at noon," I replied, wondering what was going on.

I was about to hang up when Gloria asked, "Would you mind if I bring a girlfriend?"

"That's fine, but I'll need her name for the list at the desk."

There was a pause on the other end of the phone then Gloria said, "Rosa. Rosa Russo."

When I didn't respond right away, Gloria asked, "Martha, are you still there?"

"Yes, I'm here. I'll add Rosa to the list. See you at noon." I quickly hung up, wondering if I'd made a mistake. I was stepping over the boundaries of two men I didn't particularly want to irritate—my son and our in-house gangster who hated not only me, but also the woman I was about to have lunch with. I hoped and prayed Joey would be lunching in his apartment or going early, as many men did.

—

I arrived at the dining room before the appointed time so I could get my lunch and secure an out-of-the-way table. However, when my two guests arrived, all eyes turned in their direction. Two attractive women dressed in high-heeled leather boots and short skirts were like beacons in a snowstorm at Martyn Manor. My gorgeous friend, Molly, the rare exception.

Both women had olive complexions, dark brown hair (Rosa's was obviously dyed), heavily made-up eyes, and big personalities. Although Rosa was probably at least twenty years older than Gloria, they could have been sisters.

Even though I was seated at the table, the women managed to hug me before they sashayed over to the cafeteria line. Conversation in the room ground to a halt as all eyes followed them. So much for being incognito.

Introductions had been made during the hugging, so Gloria jumped right into a conversation. "I suppose you heard that Rich and I broke up."

"No." I wasn't completely surprised by this revelation. I had figured as much when he canceled lunch. He probably didn't want to discuss his personal life. "What happened, if you don't mind my asking?"

Gloria gestured with her fork in the air. Fortunately, it wasn't full of pasta. "He was the one to break up with me. He said we weren't as compatible as he'd first thought. I didn't know what he meant by that, but I let it go. I certainly don't want to be with someone who doesn't want to be with me."

There wasn't much I could say, so I wisely kept my mouth shut.

"Even though Rich and I are no longer together, I hope you and I can still be friends. I enjoyed our lunch last month and since my mom died last year, I found it comforting to be with a mom-figure." Gloria looked at her friend. "Rosa and I are more like sisters," she added by way of explanation.

I nodded my understanding. "Since I rarely see my daughters, I'd welcome the opportunity to spend time with you as long as my son doesn't mind. I'd like to keep peace in the family."

Gloria took a big gulp of red wine. I didn't know a person could order wine at lunch. "Oh, he doesn't mind. When he called to make sure I knew that we wouldn't be coming to see you," she touched my hand, "it was on my calendar from earlier," she removed her hand and picked up her fork, "I asked him if he was going anyway. When he said he was canceling, I asked if he'd mind if I went. I figured you would be disappointed if no one came. He agreed, although to be honest, he didn't sound terribly enthusiastic.

But then Rich never sounded enthusiastic about anything." Gloria's lips turned up at the corners. "Well, maybe about one thing."

Once again, I prudently held my tongue and she continued.

"Anyway, here we are and, since I spoke about my friend last month," she smiled at Rosa, "I invited her to come along."

Rosa looked nervous, and I wondered if she thought Gloria bringing her was an imposition. "Is everything all right, Rosa? You seem nervous. By the way, I'm glad you came."

"I'm worried about seeing my ex-husband."

"I rarely see him at lunch," I reassured her.

"He's a dangerous man and he has a lot of enemies." Rosa leaned toward me. "In fact, I wouldn't be surprised if someone doesn't knock him off one of these days…if you know what I mean."

"I know what you mean."

Rosa sat back in her chair. "Frankly, I hope it's sooner than later. This world would be a better place without him and," smile lines crinkled at the corners of her eyes, "he's probably forgotten to take me off his life insurance policy."

"I can't say I wish someone would 'knock him off' as you suggest, but I wouldn't mind if he disappeared from Martyn Manor," I said.

Just then, Rosa's eyes grew wide and I sensed a hostile presence coming up behind me.

"Rosa! What the hell are you doing here?" Joey shouted, approaching our table.

To her credit, Rosa spoke in a calm, quiet voice. "I'm having lunch with two friends. Go away and leave us alone."

Joey pointed at me as he continued to address Rosa. "That damn woman ruined my life and here you are eating lunch with her. Do you even know who she is?"

"Yes, her name is Martha Anderson."

The dining room manager approached our table. "Is there a problem here?" he asked us.

Since I was the resident, I felt it was my responsibility to speak up. "Yes, ahh, I'm sorry but I've forgotten your name."

"Mr. Hawks."

"Oh yes, Mr. Hawks. Please escort Mr. Russo from our table. He's interrupting our lunch."

Mr. Hawks took Joey's elbow but he roughly pulled away. "You don't have to get pushy. I'm leavin'."

"Thank you, Mr. Hawks. Please see that he continues to keep his distance," I said.

"Of course, Mrs. Anderson." Mr. Hawks walked away with a straight back and a long stride. He probably thought he'd just saved three damsels in distress.

Rosa turned to Gloria. "Now you understand what I've been complaining about and why I wouldn't mind if someone evaporated him."

She looked over at me. "It sounds like you know Joey rather well, Martha."

There was a pregnant pause while I thought about what and how much to say. "I can't say that I personally know Joey, but as you may know, I was instrumental in getting him arrested for illegally entering my apartment and setting off false fire alarms."

I gave Gloria a serious look. "Richard doesn't know about my involvement in all this, and I'd like to keep it that way."

Gloria ran her finger over her lips, reminding me of my granddaughter when we made a pledge that what happened on our cruise stayed on our cruise.

"My lips are sealed," Gloria promised. "Anyway, I doubt very much if I'll be talking with him in the future."

"Thank you. My son can be overprotective at times. I don't want to give him any reason to consider moving me to another location. I'm settled and I want to live here for the rest of my days."

"I understand. I can tell that you're much more, shall we say, adventurous, than your son. Sometime I'd," she looked over at Rosa, "we'd like to hear your Joey story. Wouldn't we, Rosa?"

"We certainly would!" Rosa replied. "I can't believe you have to live under the same roof with that man. I'm glad you took him down. I'm sure he had it coming!"

I was aware that conversations in the dining room had quieted. Unfortunately, our trio seemed to be the lunchtime entertainment.

To steer us in another direction, I asked, "Tell me about yourself, Rosa. All I know is that you and Gloria grew up in Brooklyn and now you live in the same condo complex."

Rosa didn't offer much more than what I already knew. She and Joey had no children, although Joey had a son by a previous marriage. They divorced after abruptly moving to Poughkeepsie. She thought he had money hidden away. She greatly resented this as she was forced to live on little more than her monthly Social Security check and a small pension. She assured me that she wouldn't be homeless because she owned her condo but her social activities were curtailed due to her lack of funds.

It was all a little too personal for a first meeting, but this level of intimacy seemed to be normal for these two ladies.

With the mention of social activities, Gloria spoke up. "I think the three of us should make plans to go to Maloney's. How expensive can a round of beer be anyway? Is there a cover charge during the week, Martha?"

"No cover charge. Burgers are inexpensive, greasy, and good. Beer on tap is cheap. I'm a beer drinker myself." I looked from one lady to the other. "I'd be willing to tag along if you two decide to go."

After saying this, I wondered if I was ready to return without Missy and my other friends. I guessed it was time to find out. This was an opportunity to have some fun and get away from the Manor for an evening.

By the time lunch was over, plans were made for the following Wednesday. Rosa and Gloria agreed to pick me up at six o'clock.

I returned to my apartment and put a Post-it note by the door so I wouldn't forget our date. I was looking forward to a greasy dinner and a glass of beer with two youngish women.

—

When Harold picked me up for dinner, his demeanor was cold. Even before we got to the elevator, he said, "I heard you had lunch today with Joey's ex-wife. How in the world did THAT happen?"

Since Harold was so unhappy with my lunchtime companion, I decided not to tell him about our future outing to Maloney's. I wouldn't be going to dinner that night, so I'd have to eventually let him know, but now was definitely not the time.

I explained about meeting Richard's now ex-girlfriend last month, and how she happened to be friends with Rosa because they lived in the same building and they both grew up in Brooklyn. I asked how he happened to know about their visit.

"Because Joey stormed into the shop and asked me why the hell my friend Martha was having lunch with The Devil. Once I decoded his message and realized that The Devil was his ex-wife, I explained to him that I wasn't related to you in any way and I didn't keep track of your luncheon companions."

"Did that satisfy him?" I asked cautiously.

"I guess so. He stormed out without saying another word. But it doesn't bode well for you that he's so upset. You've really stirred up a hornet's nest." Harold gave me his stern military man look.

We exited the elevator and sat down at our usual table. After we ordered our dinners, I tried to explain myself. "I didn't have lunch with Rosa to stir Joey up if that's what you're thinking. After Richard canceled his usual monthly lunch, Gloria called to see if she could come and bring a friend. It wasn't until after I'd agreed to her request that I found out the friend was Rosa. It was all innocent on my part, although I can understand why Joey wouldn't see it that way. In fact, he made a scene in the dining room and Mr. Hawks had to escort him out."

Harold took a gulp of his burgundy then set it back down. "Good grief!"

"And how was your day…besides the interlude with Joey?" I asked, trying to take the heat off of my somewhat questionable decisions.

"Fine."

I knew Harold was miffed, but I figured he'd soon come around because it was meatloaf night and he loved meatloaf.

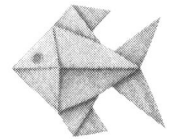

Chapter Ten

I was riding the stationary bicycle in the workout room and thinking about my Wednesday outing with Gloria and Rosa, when I realized I hadn't been this excited about something since my granddaughter's wedding.

If a person wasn't careful, life in assisted living could boil down to meals and Bingo. It had been nearly two years since my Gang of Five and I were going on clandestine outings and solving crimes.

Bored had never been in my vocabulary and I wasn't about to end my days staring at four walls. These two women were my ticket to a more fun-filled life.

Gloria and Rosa were probably not the type of women I'd choose to be my bosom buddies but they offered a change of pace from those around me who were mostly feeble in body or mind. I valued my friendship with Laura, but she certainly wasn't a candidate for karaoke night at a college bar.

—

On Wednesday morning I notified Judy, who had recently been promoted to Assisted Living Director, that I'd be off premises for the evening. When she asked me for details, I told her I was going to Maloney's with two women I'd met through my son. I promised her I'd return by nine o'clock. I hated feeling like a watched-over teenager, but I was getting accustomed to the age-reversal that comes with growing old.

—

That afternoon, I texted Harold that I wouldn't be going to dinner, he tagged my text with a question mark and I replied.

> *I'm going out to dinner with Rosa and Gloria. I'll ask one of them to walk me to my apartment when we return.*

Harold didn't reply. He just tagged my text with a thumbs up. I knew he wasn't happy about the arrangement. Richard also wouldn't appreciate my going to Mahoney's, much less with Gloria, but it was extremely unlikely that he'd be there on karaoke night, so I wasn't worried.

—

Two hours later, I pulled my black and white polka dot blouse from my closet. My granddaughter, Barbara, gave it to me for Christmas. She knew polka dots made me smile. Fortunately, the matching black skinny jeans were also on the hanger, so I had no additional decisions to make. I added my sneakers that looked like flats, refreshed my makeup, fluffed up my hair, and made my way to the front door. I was a little worried about my trip downstairs since Harold normally escorted me at that time of day, but I arrived with no untimely detours.

The girls were prompt. Gloria came in, took me by the elbow, walked me to the car, and settled me into the front seat next to Rosa, who was driving.

When we entered Mahoney's, I was completely taken aback when the hostess remembered me. "It's so good to see you again. It's been a long time," the young lady said as she grabbed menus from her podium. "I see you have new friends with you tonight."

"Nice of you to remember me," I replied. "Would you mind seating us over there?" I pointed to the booth on the opposite side of the room from the one where Missy and I had sat together for our romantic evening nearly two years ago.

"Of course. Right this way, ladies."

I sat down opposite my friends, who were staring at me. "What?" I asked.

"I thought you were only here for your birthday party," Gloria replied.

"I might have been here once or twice more. They were rather memorable occasions that apparently stuck with the staff," I offered matter-of-factly. I hoped our waiter was new. "By the way, I highly recommend the onion rings."

When our server approached, he looked at me then at my companions. "And where is the lovely lady with the voice of an angel?" he asked.

I felt my face grow red as I fought back tears. "Unfortunately, she died last year."

Sounding genuinely sad, he said, "I'm so sorry for your loss." He looked at my companions. "Do either of you ladies sing?"

Rosa gave him what my dad would call a come-hither look. "With enough alcohol, we might."

The guy smiled back. He'd probably heard that one before.

We ordered our burgers, onion rings, and beers.

Midway through our dinner, someone stepped up to sing. College kids were filling up the place and my two friends no longer seemed so young. In fact, it seemed to me that they were trying too hard to look hip. It probably wasn't easy for women their age to find eligible bachelors.

After a second beer, Gloria signed up for karaoke. When she returned to the table, I asked about her song choice.

"You'll see," she said coyly.

I was quite certain it wouldn't be "Moon River," the romantic song Missy dedicated to me when we were an item.

Gloria stepped onto the stage and the audience quieted. She was old for this crowd, but she was still attractive, and her short skirt showed off her lovely legs.

She sang "Candle In The Wind," an Elton John classic about Marilyn Monroe. Her voice wasn't angelic like Missy's, but it was good and she sat down to a big round of applause. As when Missy sang, an order of fries showed up at our table. Since the onion ring orders were small, we had room for the fries and they disappeared in minutes.

The music and conversation were loud, so there wasn't much chit-chat which was just as well since I didn't want to discuss my past. We listened to a couple of singers, then I asked our waiter for the check.

After I paid the bill, Gloria said, "You didn't have to do that, Martha."

"It's my way of thanking you for taking an old lady out for a fun evening. I enjoyed our time together," I said as I gathered up my things. "Now it's time I get back before they send the bloodhounds after me."

My two companions smiled. Little did they know how close the statement was to the truth.

After Gloria safely escorted me to my apartment, I texted Harold and the person on night duty to let them know I had returned. Harold only responded with a thumbs-up. Apparently, he was still miffed about my "risky" behavior.

—

The next morning I was buttering my English muffin when I looked up to see Joey glaring at me from across the table.

"Stay away from my ex-wife," he hissed. "Or else!"

"Or else what?" I asked.

"Just stay out of my life. Believe me, you don't want to know the 'or else'." He placed his elbows on the table and leaned across so he could look me in the eyes. "Kapeesh?"

I nodded, but I wasn't about to back down. I held his gaze and gave him a steely look. "Last I heard, this is a free country."

Without responding, Joey abruptly left my table, stomped across the room, and out the door.

I let out a big breath I didn't know I was holding. I wondered if they vetted people before they accepted them into this place, or did they take anyone who had the entrance fee and could prove they were good for the monthly payments.

Before I could return to my green tea, Ethyl slid into the seat Joey had just vacated. I liked to eat breakfast alone and my patience with unwanted and uninvited guests had worn thin.

"What do you want?" I asked Ethyl.

"Since when do you hobnob with Joey Russo?"

"I wasn't hobnobbing. He sat down without an invitation—just like someone else I know." I gave her a look that indicated she needed to leave.

"He certainly didn't look happy. What do you know about him?" When I didn't respond, she continued. "If he's an old friend of Ralph Jensen's, he's trouble," Ethyl said without giving any indication she was about to leave.

"What do YOU know about Joey?" I asked in return. If I had to deal with my nosy neighbor at breakfast, I might as well come away with something.

"Since he's been here, Russo's been arrested and he's serving out his sentence..." she paused for emphasis, "in his apartment!"

I waved my hand. "I know all that. What else do you know?"

"What's it worth to you?" Ethyl gave me a haughty look.

"What do you have in mind?"

"Dinner at Maloney's."

Good grief! This woman was persistent.

"Maybe…." I hedged.

"Wednesday," she countered.

"Wednesday is karaoke and it's too loud to talk. How about Sunday? No karaoke, but the onion rings are still amazing," I offered. I wondered why I was agreeing to this. I'd be spending an evening with a woman I could barely tolerate.

"Sunday it is. You set up the Uber. I'll meet you at the front door at six o'clock. You better be there!"

"Are you threatening me?" I narrowed my eyes at her. "Do you want to go to Maloney's or not? If we're going to do this, you need to be civil." I wasn't about to let Joey OR Ethyl bully me.

"Sorry. See you on Sunday," she said as contritely as was possible for Ethyl.

—

At lunch, I told Laura about my breakfast encounter with Joey and his veiled threat. She pursed her lips. "I don't like the sound of that," she said. "Have you told Harold yet?"

"I may omit that story when I see him at dinner. He'd say, 'I told you to stay out of Joey's life,' and he'd insist that I not see his ex-wife again."

Laura took a sip from her cup. She drank black tea with milk, which was quite English of her. "Sounds like a man who cares about your well-being."

"He does care, but I really had a good time with Gloria and Rosa, even though they aren't exactly my type of ladies. The thing I'm wondering about is how," I leaned in, "the hell did Joey find out that I was out with his ex?"

Laura drew her brows together. "Hmmm, that is a mystery. Maybe someone at the desk told him or he saw you leave. Maybe his ex said something just to irritate him since you're his nemesis, or maybe he has a spy in this place."

"Perhaps. I think I'll text Gloria and ask her if she knows anything about Rosa telling Joey we were together. Gloria has no skin in the game. I think she'd be honest with me."

"Good idea," Laura said before moving on to telling me about an interesting book she was reading.

—

On my way to Bingo that afternoon, I spotted another strange man walking down the hall. This one was the opposite of Ralph. He was a little shorter than average, slim, had a slight limp, and I guessed he was in his mid-sixties. When he stopped to dig around in his pocket, presumably to locate the key to the visitors' apartment, I sidled up to him. Seeing him up close, I gave a little gasp. He looked exactly like Joey Russo, just twenty years younger.

"Hello, I'm Martha Anderson. I don't believe we've met," I offered.

I was surprised when I saw a smile of recognition cross his face. "Ah, the infamous Mrs. Anderson. So, you're the person who got my dad arrested a while back."

"That's me." I could see no point in denying it. At least he wasn't hostile. In fact, he seemed downright friendly.

"Well, he certainly deserved it. He's gotten away with a lot of crap in his time."

"And you're here visiting him?" I asked. It seemed odd he'd want to visit his dad, considering he had such a low opinion of him.

"I am. Thought we should reconnect. It's been a long time."

"I don't believe I got your name," I said.

"People call me JR but to be exact, the name's Joseph Russo, Junior. I try to keep my full name under wraps—if you know what I mean."

I gave him an innocent look. "And why would that be, JR?"

"My dad has a reputation in Brooklyn that I would rather not be associated with." JR looked at me closely. "But you already know that, don't you?"

"Maybe…" I paused then asked, "So all of a sudden you're wanting to associate with your wayward dad?"

"There are extenuating circumstances." He finally pulled the key from his pocket. "Now, if you'll excuse me…" JR unlocked his door. "Nice meeting you, Mrs. Anderson."

"Likewise," I said and continued walking down the hall. When I got to Bingo, I texted Harold.

> You'll never guess who I just met.

Who? 🙄

> Joey's son. Joseph Russo, Jr. Otherwise known as JR.

You're kidding me.

> Nope. I'll tell you about it at dinner. Gotta go. Bingo is starting. I'm feeling lucky. 😊

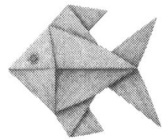

Chapter Eleven

After winning five dollars and a box of note cards at Bingo, I was feeling good.

"How come you're so giddy tonight?" Harold asked, sensing my mood when he picked me up for dinner.

I explained about my winnings, then I told him about my visits with JR and Ethyl. Harold seemed interested. Perhaps I was back in his good graces.

"How was your outing with the girls?" he asked after our dinners were served.

"Fine. Thanks for asking."

"Fine? That's all you got?"

"Gloria sang karaoke and got a big applause. It was too loud to talk, so there was no mention of Joey, if that's what you're wondering," I said as I forked a succulent bite of broiled salmon into my mouth. Seafood was a treat because it was rarely served.

Then right out of the blue, Harold said, "Joey's making a metal canister. He's very secretive about his project but I happened to notice it when I walked by."

"Wow, that's interesting intel. What do you think it's for?" I asked.

"I've been considering that question all afternoon. Perhaps it's to hide rolled-up bills or precious stones." Harold looked at me. When I remained quiet, he added, "I have a feeling it has something to do with his possible stash. Or" Harold gave me a mischievous look, "he's making an ashtray like I used to make for my dad at Christmas back in the day."

"So, you agree with the premise that he participated in a bank heist and has money hidden away?" I wanted Harold to commit.

"Possibly."

—

The following morning there was a ruckus outside Judy's office. I slowly walked by to see if I could catch the drift of what was happening. In addition to Judy, Joey was there along with a cleaning lady and a nursing assistant. I figured they were standing in the hall since Judy only had two extra chairs in her office.

"When did you discover your apartment had been ransacked?" Judy asked Joey.

"This morning. I went to breakfast early, just like I always do and when I got back to my place, it was a mess. Drawers open, cushions tossed all over, bed stripped. What kind of place you runnin' here anyways?"

Judy ignored his question and asked the ladies if they'd seen any suspicious people in the hallways. Both shook their heads no. I wasn't able to hear the rest of the conversation because Judy gave me a look that told me to move on and mind my own business. She can be tough when necessary.

I texted Harold as soon as I got to the dining room.

> You had breakfast yet?

No, why?

> Come on down. I'll wait for you.

?

> Just come!

Not five minutes later, I saw Harold enter the dining room and pick up cereal and coffee. Since he was bypassing his usual omelet or waffle, I figured he was really curious.

"What's up?" he asked as he pulled out his chair.

"Sit down. I have news."

Harold dutifully sat down and blew on his coffee. "Well?"

I looked around to make sure no one was listening. "On my way here, I overheard Judy talking to Joey. Apparently, while he was at breakfast, his apartment was tossed."

"You're kidding me."

"Nope. Judy had one of the cleaning ladies and an assistant there to ask them if they'd seen anyone coming or going."

"And?"

"They said they hadn't."

Harold put a spoonful of Cheerios in his mouth. After he swallowed, he said, "You sound like you don't believe them."

"I have no reason to doubt them, but it seems strange that someone could toss Joey's apartment so early in the morning and in such a short span of time. Heck, he's only at breakfast for about a half hour tops, which includes coming and going."

Harold stroked his stubbled chin. Apparently, I'd lured him out of his apartment before he'd had time to shave. "It wouldn't take long. Joey has a studio. Basically, it's one room and a bathroom. Maybe they were looking for the stash."

"My thoughts exactly. Will you ask him about it? Say you heard about what happened to his apartment and see what he says."

"Why do I always feel like Batman's Robin?"

I gave him a little kick under the table. "Isn't that better than being the Joker?"

Harold smiled. "Finish your Grape-Nuts. I'll walk you to the workout room, then I'll start my stakeout at the shop." He shook his head. "It's gonna be a long day."

—

It was a long day for me, too, because I was counting down the hours until dinner. I figured Harold wouldn't text me unless it was urgent. He'd rather wait and give me the intel in person. I was waiting outside my door when Harold arrived at dinnertime. "Well?"

"Good grief! You got ants in your pants?" he asked.

I started walking. "I've been waiting all day to find out what you learned."

"You'll have to wait a few more minutes."

It was Italian night. Harold ordered lasagna and I ordered angel hair pasta with marinara sauce. We each had a glass of Chianti. I was reminded of my Italian dinners with Susan on the cruise. I was trying to distract myself from the question of the day, which was 'what did Joey say?'

While we waited for our entrees to arrive, Harold spoke quietly. "When I asked Joey about his apartment and if he knew who did it or why, he said he didn't know. Then…" Harold took a drink of wine.

I held my tongue. Believe me, it wasn't easy!

"He said he thought someone was out to kill him."

Just then our dinners were served, and I was left with my mouth hanging open. I'm not sure it was literally open, but it felt that way. When the server left I asked, "As in murder?"

"Yes!" Harold shout-whispered.

"I'm surprised he confided in you."

"I think he's lonely and depressed. He has no friends here and it sounds like he burned all his bridges from his past life. He probably needs someone to talk to and since I'm always handy," Harold gave me a pointed look, "he's starting to open up and trust me with his personal business."

"See? What did I tell you?" I couldn't help myself.

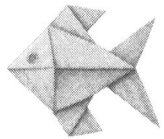

Chapter Twelve

By Wednesday, I was regretting telling Ethel I'd go to Mahoney's with her. I was also increasingly worried about Joey's threat. Would he really do something to me? Was he as dangerous as his ex-wife and Ethyl seemed to think? It was a boring day, and I had too much time to think. I also heard from Gloria that Rosa had no idea how Joey might have known I was out to dinner with them. I felt like I was being watched.

—

After lunch, I was settling down in my recliner to listen to my book and embroider, when I heard the shriek of sirens followed by feet thundering down the hall. By the time I got to the door to look out, the commotion was over.

I settled back in my chair and resumed listening to my book, figuring I'd hear the scuttlebutt about what happened at dinner. Twenty minutes later, there was a loud knock on my door. I called out, "Door's open, come in."

As soon as the words were out of my mouth, I regretted saying them. I had to remind myself that I could be in danger. Thankfully, it was Ethyl who came stomping in.

"What are you doing here?" I asked. Uninvited visitors were definitely a no-no at the Manor.

Ethyl turned back toward the door. "Well, if you don't want to know what happened…."

"Wait," I said. "You mean the sirens and commotion down the hall?"

"Yes."

"Sit down."

Ethyl settled herself on my love seat. "Got anything to drink?"

She could be so uncouth. I pointed to the mini fridge. "Help yourself." After getting her soda, she sat back down.

"Well?"

"Joey Russo's dead. I think he was murdered," Ethyl said nonchalantly, like there was a murder at Martyn Manor every day.

"Murdered!" I shouted.

"Yes, murdered." Ethyl took a drink of her soda. "If you'll simmer down, I'll tell you about it. I was fortunate to be in the vicinity when he was found. I stayed until after the EMTs and police showed up."

"Lucky you."

"Wanna know more or not?"

"Spill it."

"Well…"

Like Harold, Ethyl enjoyed milking a good story.

"An aide periodically checks on Joey during the day because he has some kind of fainting condition."

I interrupted. "He has syncope. He's also a diabetic."

"Whatever." She waved her hand. "So just as I happened to be walking by his apartment, I looked through the partially open door to see Jimmy, the new orderly, leaning over a body on the floor. He lifted Joey's legs, and when he didn't come to, Jimmy checked for a pulse. Apparently, he found none because he immediately called 911 and pulled Russo's emergency cord."

"You found all this out drifting by his apartment?"

"By then, I had drifted, as you say, into the apartment and offered my assistance. Jimmy was very distraught, so he didn't mind that I was there. He even asked me to bring him a glass of water."

"Go on." I wanted to know why she thought Joey was murdered.

"When the EMTs arrived, they declared him dead and called the police because they noticed an overturned glass of reddish liquid near his body. They sniffed the liquid, then decided to wait for the authorities before moving Russo."

"Did you smell anything?"

Ethyl thought for a minute. "Now that you ask, there was a bitter almond scent in the room. I thought it was an air freshener, but maybe not."

"Hmmm." I thought about googling the scent but I didn't want to interrupt Ethyl's story. "No one asked you to leave?"

"I made myself invisible. You know how easy that is for us old ladies." When she looked over at me, I nodded in the affirmative. "Anyway, they probably thought I was his wife or something; although you'd think they would have noticed that I wasn't crying or carrying on."

"So, you were still there when the police arrived?"

"Yes. By then, Judy and several other staff members had entered the room. Do you know that he lives, correction, lived, in a studio?"

"Yes."

"It's tiny." Ethyl took another drink of her soda. "Just before they put Russo in a body bag and hoisted him onto a gurney, a detective showed up, examined the body, and also sniffed the spilled liquid."

"Then what?"

"About that time, Judy spotted me and, in no uncertain terms, told me to get out and to keep all that I'd seen and heard under wraps. On my way down the hall, I saw that plainclothes detective that I've seen you talking to in the past. Apparently, he saw me exiting Russo's apartment because he also told me to keep my mouth shut. He's scary."

"Yet, here you are."

Ethyl gave me a shrewd look. "As much as you're not my favorite person," she looked to see my response. I nodded my understanding and she continued. "I don't want you to succumb to whatever happened to Russo. People know you've been nosing around and were the one who got him arrested. I wanted to warn you in case your life is in danger."

"Thanks for your concern," I said with sincerity. "Anything else?"

Ethyl got up, threw the empty soda can in my garbage, then turned toward the door. "That's all I've got for now. I'll keep you posted."

"You do that."

Ethyl turned and smiled before closing my door. "See you Sunday." Obviously, she hadn't forgotten about our outing.

I sat back in my chair and pulled out my phone. I sent an email to myself reminding me to look up what substance smells like bitter almond. It seemed like a unique combination.

There was a lot to process. I decided to wait until dinner to tell Harold the news, although I was sure he'd hear about it before then.

Chapter Thirteen

Just as I was changing for dinner, there was another loud knock. I quickly threw a dress over my head and rushed to the door, mindful of my earlier mistake of allowing a potential stranger to enter my apartment without me checking them out. When I opened the door a crack, I looked up to see the ominous form of Detective Warren with his sidekick, Detective Niles, standing just behind him.

I'd had several dealings with Warren since moving to Martyn Manor, including him accusing me of Harold's disappearance, helping him catch a purse snatcher, identifying Duly as a thief, plus the Russo case. We had quite a history.

"We need to talk," Warren said without offering a howdy-do or asking if he could come in. He wore his usual black suit, but it was wrinkled as though he'd slept in it. His tie was askew, and there was a prominent spot on his otherwise white shirt.

My only response was to open the door wider. The two detectives filed in. Warren was a big man; Niles was a small woman. Warren pulled a chair out from the table and brought it to the living room. Besides his untidy appearance, he had dark circles under his eyes, and his hair was uncustomarily long. Niles, who looked tidy as usual, took the love seat, and I sat in my recliner.

"What's this about?" I asked.

"Joey Russo's dead. Possibly poisoned," Warren said.

"So I heard."

That remark got his attention. "How did YOU find out?" he demanded.

"You have your sources, I have mine." I gave Warren a slight smile but he didn't smile back. "How can I help you? Harold will be here any minute to escort me to dinner. Let's get this over with."

Niles spoke up. She was more cordial. They were a good-cop, bad-cop team. "We're here to ask you some preliminary questions, Mrs. Anderson. Tomorrow, we'd like you to come to the station for a more in-depth interview."

My heart started pounding. Did they think I murdered Russo? Was I an easy target in their investigation? Did I need a lawyer?

"Ask away," I offered, trying to sound nonchalant.

"Where were you this afternoon about two thirty?" Warren asked, wiping the sweat from his brow with a crumpled handkerchief.

"Right here."

"Was anyone with you?" Niles asked.

"No. I was alone until about twenty minutes after the sirens and the noise in the hall died down, then my neighbor, Ethyl Haggerty, stopped by."

Warren started writing in a notebook he pulled from his vest pocket. "I see."

"How well did you know Joey Russo?" Niles asked.

"Do I need to remind you of our history?"

"I suppose not," she replied. When Warren grunted, Niles gave him a side-eye glance.

"We've never had a friendly relationship, if that's what you're asking." I sat back in the recliner, resigned to the fact that I was going to be there for a while.

Warren leaned forward in his chair. He seemed fidgety and in a hurry to move on. "We've had reports that he accosted you more than once in the dining room. Is that true?"

"Yes. He interrupted a lunch I was having with his ex-wife and another friend of mine. Mr. Hawks, the dining room manager, intervened. More recently, he threatened me at breakfast."

Flipping the page of his notebook, Warren asked, "How did he threaten you? What exactly did he say?"

"He said I needed to stay away from his ex-wife or else. He refused to define the 'or else.' Russo wasn't a nice man, Detective. As you probably know, he had a long history of trouble in Brooklyn, so I imagine you have a list of suspects in his possible murder. I'd suggest you get on with your investigation and let me go to dinner."

Warren got up from his chair and hastily put the notebook back in his pocket. "You're also on that list, Mrs. Anderson." He gave me a stern look, his dark eyes menacing. "You're not planning another transcontinental cruise, are you?"

I wondered how he knew about the trip where I'd actually witnessed a murder, but decided not to ask. "No. I won't be going any further than the local library."

"Good. We'll send a squad car tomorrow morning to take you to the station. I'll text you the time."

With that, Warren, followed by Niles, exited my apartment.

I let out a long sigh. I was too old for intense conversations with the police, to say nothing of being a potential suspect in a murder investigation.

I was putting on my jewelry when I heard a tap on the door, then Harold called out, "It's just me."

"Martha, you've got to keep your door locked," I muttered to myself before hollering, "I'll be out in a minute."

"No rush."

When I slowly exited my bedroom, Harold took one look at me and said, "What's up? You look done in."

"Thanks," I replied.

"I take that back," Harold said. "You look as lovely as ever, but a little tired around the eyes." He smiled at me. "Better?"

"Yes." I took my key from the hook and opened the door. "I'm bushed. I'll explain at dinner."

Harold took my arm and tucked it into his as we made our way to the dining room. After we'd ordered, I named my three afternoon visitors.

"No wonder you're done in. Ethyl, Warren, and Niles. That's a combo that would take the wind out of anyone's sails."

Most of the time, Harold was very affirming. I appreciated that about him.

"That's me. Luffing in the breeze."

"You've sailed?" Harold asked.

"I've done a lot of things you don't know about, Colonel," I said before continuing with my tale of woe. "Warren was there because he has me on the list of suspects for the possible murder of Joey Russo."

"Joey Russo's been murdered?" Harold exclaimed. When heads turned our way, he leaned in. "Good grief, Martha. So that's why you had the strange visitors. What's the story, and how in the world did you get involved?"

"I thought you would have heard about Joey by now. Let's go to my place after dinner and I'll fill you in."

Harold nodded. I could tell he was still in a state of shock. "You always keep me on my toes. I was wondering when something was going to happen that you were involved in. It's been a while."

"I know. I was getting bored but…" I whispered, "murder suspect is more than I bargained for."

Our dinner arrived and we settled down to eat. After Harold had a few sips of wine, I asked, "Will you accompany me to the police station tomorrow?"

He made a little choking sound. "Of course, but why the station? I thought they questioned you this afternoon in your apartment."

"According to Detective Niles, that was only a preliminary interview. Warren is sending a squad car to pick me up in the morning. He's going to text me the time."

"This feels like déjà vu, only the last time you were at the station, it was to help solve a crime, not because you were a suspect in one."

"Have you forgotten that I was a suspect in your disappearance?" I took the last bite of my cherry pie. It was my second favorite next to lemon meringue. "Maybe this will be an opportunity for me to gather information and help solve this case."

Harold gave me his 'mind your own business' look. "Maybe."

"By the way," I added, thinking out loud, "Warren didn't look himself at all. His clothes were disheveled and he looked tired. I don't mean one-bad-night's-sleep tired. I mean at-the-end-of-his-rope tired. It made me wonder what's going on with him."

"Good grief, Martha. Isn't one mystery at a time enough for you?"

I got up from the table. "You're right. I'll make an effort to keep my eye on the ball."

When we returned to my apartment, I filled Harold in on the details of what Ethyl told me and my interview with the detectives.

"I wonder what they have on you to go to the trouble to bring you down to the station?" Harold asked. He was always a step ahead of me. He still had the mind of a combat leader.

"Hmmm. I didn't think of that. I guess we'll find out."

Harold steepled his fingers. "I wonder if the killer was looking for the stash?"

I pondered the question for a minute. "And, if so, did he," I paused for a minute, "or she find it?"

Chapter Fourteen

After Harold and I were escorted to the interrogation room and sat down, I looked around. Same battered table from when we'd been there before, but the walls had been painted. Today, the air smelled more like fresh paint than unwashed bodies.

Detective Warren, with Niles in tow, greeted us with a grunt. "You didn't tell me HE was coming," he said, looking at Harold.

"You mean Mr. Lancaster?"

Warren nodded before he pushed the button on the recorder in the middle of the table. He didn't look as wrinkled as before, but he had stubble on his jaw and his hair still needed a good trim.

"Well, you didn't ask. He's not exactly a stranger to you. He's the missing person you couldn't locate. Remember?" What was I doing stirring up the detective who had me on his suspects' list in a potential murder case? The older I got, the crankier I became toward inept people like Warren.

The detective turned to Harold. "It's good you're here. I have a few questions for you, too. I understand you and the deceased were friends."

"Acquaintances." Harold knew the rules about short answers.

Warren narrowed his eyes. I noticed that the dark circles were even more prominent than earlier. "From what my deputies tell me, you're the only person at Martyn Manor who spoke with Mr. Russo on a regular basis."

When Harold didn't respond, he changed his tactic and asked a direct question in a neutral tone. "Is there anything you can tell me about Russo and his last days?"

"I think he was depressed. He was making something out of metal. Perhaps a canister of some sort." Harold crossed his arms over his chest.

"That's it? That's all you got?"

Harold sat back in his chair. "I'm afraid so. We weren't friends, simply two guys working in the same shop who spoke from time to time."

When Warren didn't immediately follow-up, it was Harold's turn to ask a question. "What makes you think Martha had anything to do with Russo's death? And has it definitely been determined that he was murdered?"

Warren was momentarily at a loss for words and Harold was scowling, so Niles jumped in. "Mrs. Anderson was invited here because of remarks she made about Mr. Russo that were overheard by certain Martyn Manor residents."

Invited? What the hell! I didn't say it, but I sure thought it.

"Thank you," Harold said politely, even though no one answered his question about whether or not Joey was murdered. Maybe we were also playing good-cop, bad-cop. "Would either of you like to elaborate on the nature of those remarks?"

Warren addressed Harold's question while glaring at me. "Several residents overheard your friend Rosa Russo, Mr. Russo's ex-wife, saying that she wouldn't mind seeing Joey bumped off, to which you responded that you'd like to see him gone from the Manor. Are these statements correct?"

"Basically, yes." I decided it was unwise to say more. Trying to defend myself could make me look guilty.

"And it seems that you're familiar with Mr. Russo's son, JR, and also a friend from his past, Ralph Jensen. Is that true?"

"Yes, but what does my knowing them have to do with me being a suspect in his potential murder?" Before he could answer, I added, "It's my job to get to know new people. I'm an official ambassador for the Manor."

Warren ignored my question and comment. "We also have evidence that you've been digging up information on Mr. Russo's past. Is this true?"

"Yes." I figured he probably wouldn't reveal his sources, but I asked the question anyway. "Who have you been speaking with?"

By way of answering my question, Warren said, "Mr. Russo's son, Mr. Jensen, and a few of your fellow residents..." he gave me a hard look, his left eye twitching, "there are any number of people who suggested we speak with you."

"What's my motive for killing Joey? It seems that JR, Ralph, Rosa, as well as other people from Joey's past all have excellent motives and yet, here I am sitting in your interrogation room. Is it because I'm an easy target, Detective Warren?" I boldly suggested.

Warren's eyes narrowed and his bristly chin jutted out. I had hit a nerve. Either that or he was fed up with my impertinence.

He asked a few other inane questions, like had I seen any strangers in the halls the day Russo died, then he circled back to my so-called relationship with Russo.

"I did not have a personal relationship with Mr. Russo," I explained. "I met his ex-wife through a mutual friend. I didn't seek her out because of her relationship with Mr. Russo. I didn't like Russo, and I didn't like having a felon living at Martyn Manor, but I certainly didn't poison him." I figured I'd float the theory in order to observe Warren's response.

"Poison? Who said anything about poison?" Warren shouted.

"I heard through the grapevine that he might have been poisoned. Was he?" I asked.

Warren slapped his hands on the table. "That is none of your business, Mrs. Anderson!"

I jumped at the slap then casually asked, "Are we done here?"

"For now," hissed Warren before abruptly leaving the room.

"We'll have a squad car take you back to the Manor. Wait here a moment," said Niles.

Since her look was sympathetic, her voice kind, I asked, "How long will it take before they know if Russo was poisoned or not?"

"It could take a while," Niles explained. "The medical examiner is backed up and they've called in a forensic pathologist."

When she left the room, Harold looked at me. "You're one feisty woman, Mrs. Anderson."

"I'll take that as a compliment, Colonel. Now, get me out of here!"

On the way home, I pulled the scrap of paper with the warning to mind my own business from my pocket and handed it to Harold.

"When did you get this?" he asked, narrowing his eyes at me.

"A few weeks ago." I grimaced, knowing Harold was going to be angry and disappointed that I'd kept the note from him.

Rather than chastise me, he asked, "Why didn't you show this to Warren?"

"Since I'm ninety-nine percent sure it was from Russo, I didn't see the point. And, it might have given him more ammunition to keep me on his suspects list."

Harold handed the note back to me, shook his head slowly from side to side, and closed his eyes. He was probably trying to control his temper.

"And what about the one percent? Have you thought about that?"

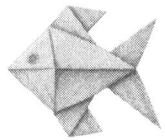

Chapter Fifteen

Sunday quickly rolled around and I went to Maloney's with Ethyl as promised. The room was packed, keeping conversation to a minimum which suited me just fine. Since she had nothing new to report about the Russo case, the outing seemed redundant.

On the way home, I figured it was as good a time as any to ask Ethyl why she'd been so mean to me in the past. If we were to be partners on the Russo Case, I needed to let bygones be bygones.

"To be honest…" Ethyl paused, and I waited. "To be honest, I was jealous of you. Still am if you want to know the truth."

"Jealous? Why?" I asked.

"People referred to you and your friends as the Sensational Six, and I wasn't a part of the group."

"They did?" I asked, dumbfounded.

Ethyl explained. "Yes. You were close, you had fun, you had each other's backs, and I had nobody. Well, I had Audrey, but then she turned out to be a terrible person when she jilted Bob, so that was even worse than having no friend at all."

"I had no idea you felt that way. I can't excuse your actions toward me, but at least now I understand."

Ethyl looked over at me in the darkened car. "Do you think you can forgive me?"

I was taken aback when I saw a tear roll down her cheek. "Probably. Let's declare tonight a new start and see how it goes."

Just then, the car stopped in front of the Manor and we got out. "I'll walk you to your apartment, Martha. Thanks for going with me to Maloney's," Ethyl said as we walked into the building together.

—

The story of Joey Russo's death and possible murder spread like wildfire throughout Martyn Manor. It seemed that everyone was suddenly an amateur detective speculating on the cause of his death and, if he was murdered, who did it and how.

More than once, eyes turned toward me in the dining room as people discussed "the case." I hated being under suspicion and the subject of "table talk," but until the case of Joey's death was resolved, there was no way to clear my name.

—

The week after Russo's death, I was asked to meet a new move-in. I was glad for the distraction. Agatha Garett seemed nice on the phone and I was looking forward to the prospect of making another friend.

When we met outside the dining room, I was surprised by Agatha's appearance, sure that she'd once been movie-star gorgeous. She was still quite lovely with red hair, sparkling blue eyes, and pale, glowing skin. Although she used a cane, she stood straight—her boot-cut slacks and silk blouse showed off her still-shapely figure. When I saw her take an uneven step and her hand shake, I could tell that Parkinson's disease was likely what brought her to the Manor.

After a general introductory chit-chat, I asked her if she knew Joey Russo. I thought she might have known him in the past because of her pronounced Brooklyn accent. There was a distinct flicker of recognition in her eyes before she said, "The name sounds familiar. Isn't he the guy who was murdered recently?"

I told her that the cause of his death was still under investigation. She gave me a knowing look as if she, too, was suspicious about my involvement.

During our lunch, I learned she was a short-term renter like Audrey Metcaff, who was a troublemaker from the past. Then, just as I was considering whether or not to have ice cream for dessert, Agatha threw me for a loop with a bold question. "What's your relationship with Harold Lancaster? Are you sleeping with him?"

Aghast, it took me a moment to regain my composure. "What?" I asked. I was hoping I had misunderstood.

"You heard me. Are you and Harold sleeping together? Are you intimate partners?"

"What an outrageous question! The answer is no—not that it's any of your business," I said while giving her a hard look. So much for making a new friend.

"Good." Agatha popped the last bite of her tuna sandwich into her mouth. "Do they offer good prizes at Bingo?"

"Depends on what you consider good," I answered as I laid my napkin beside my plate. So much for ice cream. I wanted to terminate this lunch as soon as possible.

"It's been interesting making your acquaintance, Agatha. Now," I got up from my chair and pushed it into the table, "if you'll excuse me, I have another appointment."

On my way out of the dining room, I wondered about the intent of her question. Was it simply to rattle me? Was she looking for confirmation that Harold was available? Did she have a type of Parkinson's dementia that caused her to be unaware of what she was saying?

I walked down the hall and took the elevator up, but my addled brain told me to get off at the wrong floor, which increased my agitation. When I finally got back to my apartment and settled into my recliner, I had the beginning of a headache.

Thinking back over our conversation, I realized I'd learned little about Agatha other than her status as a short-term renter and confirmation of my suspicion that she had a Brooklyn connection.

—

That night at dinner, I asked Harold if he'd met the new woman.

"Nope."

"Are you sure?" I paused long enough for Harold to look up from his pork chop. "Red hair, tall, gorgeous, walks with a fancy cane."

"Oh, is that her name?" Harold asked.

"So, you've seen her around," I said to confirm.

"I guess so. The description sounds familiar. No one else in this place looks like that. How do you know her?"

"I had lunch with her today in my role of ambassador." I looked over at Harold. "Your name came up."

Genuinely surprised, he asked, "My name? That's odd." He resumed cutting his pork chop. "I've not met her or spoken to her. After you described her, I realized I've seen her around, but that's it."

Harold looked up from his plate with a slight twinkle in his eye. "So, what did she say about me?"

I leaned in and whispered, "She wanted to know if we were sleeping together." I sat back, waiting for Harold's reaction.

"She WHAT?" he spoke loud enough for heads to turn. Did people have nothing better to do at dinner than listen to the conversation at neighboring tables?

"Yep. That's exactly what she asked. Not long after, I left her to finish her iced tea alone. The nerve of that woman!" I felt my cheeks burning. I was still mad. "I keep telling myself that maybe she has a type of dementia and wasn't aware of her outrageous and impolite question."

Harold still looked perplexed. "How does she even know my name?"

"I have no idea." Just then, I looked to my left in time to see Agatha coming through the door of the dining room. When Harold followed my gaze, she gave him a finger wave…with me sitting right there! Harold quickly looked down at his plate.

"The audacity of that woman!" I exclaimed.

"Yeah, the audacity," said Harold under his breath.

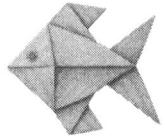

Chapter Sixteen

At lunch the next day, I saw Agatha and Ethyl eating together. If only I was a roach under the table so I could hear their conversation. I sincerely hoped they weren't becoming friends.

I returned to my apartment still feeling rattled by recent events when there was a knock. Being cautious of strangers at my door, I rose from my recliner, walked to the door, and peeked out. Ethyl stood there with her hands on her hips.

"What now?" I asked, pulling the door open.

"Wanna know what Dragon Lady said or not?"

"Dragon Lady?"

"You know. Agatha."

"Come on in."

As she settled herself on the love seat, I went to my mini fridge and pulled out a can of soda before Ethyl could ask for one.

"Thanks," she said when I handed it to her.

"Well?" I said after putting my feet up again.

Ethyl opened with, "I think she's a fake."

"What do you mean?"

"I think that walk of hers is fake and the cane is a prop. She's trying to act like she has Parkinson's, but she has no tremor in her hands when she stuffs her face with food or picks up a glass to drink."

I considered this. "Go on."

"Obviously, the hair is fake, either dyed or a wig, fake eyelashes, tattooed brows, probably fake boobs. I think the Brooklyn accent is the only genuine thing about her." She paused. "Odd don't you think?"

I nodded my affirmation, thinking Ethyl had detected a lot more than I had. "Did she say anything about Harold?"

"Harold? YOUR Harold?"

"Is there more than one Harold living here?"

Ethyl smiled mischievously. "As a matter of fact, she did."

"And?"

"She wanted to know if he was available. She called him Colonel. Is he a Colonel?"

I couldn't believe it. She hadn't talked to Harold—I believed him when he said he hadn't spoken with her—yet she knew he was a retired Colonel. "Yes. He's a retired Army Lieutenant Colonel, to be exact. But how would she know that? According to Harold, they've not spoken."

Ethyl looked at me like I was a schoolgirl. "Google, my dear, Google."

"Yes, of course." I closed my eyes for a moment as I considered the situation. Then I blurted, "He's a ninety-three-year-old man, for Heaven's sake! Why in the world is she pursuing him?" I took a calming breath. "Besides, he's taken," I added, surprising myself.

Ethyl caught me off guard with a sympathetic look. I was warming up to her. "I'm sorry, Martha. It seems as though you have an adversary living in your domain." She took a sip of soda. "As you say, Harold is an old man, but I have to admit, he's still attractive."

I rolled my eyes at her.

She continued. "I think she's after a lot more than Harold. Didn't you tell me once that you thought Russo had money stashed away from a long-ago bank heist?"

"So?"

Ethyl shrugged her shoulders. "Maybe she's here to find the stash."

"Seems reasonable," I said.

"And," Ethyl went on, "didn't you tell me that, at your request, Harold befriended Joey in the woodworking shop?"

"Yes." A light bulb finally lit up in my brain. "So, you think Agatha is after Harold because she thinks he can give her clues about the stash?"

"Bingo! Makes sense, right?"

I gave Ethyl a slight smile. "Wow, you're really good at this investigative stuff."

"Thanks. Now, tell me everything you know about Joey and his possible stash. Let's solve this mystery!" Ethyl was so animated I thought she might spring off the couch. I must admit, I also felt like a can of Coke that had just been shaken.

I took a minute to consider Ethyl's request. We'd only recently erased the past when she was my archenemy but my desire to clear my name and solve the "Joey Case" got the best of me, and I told her about Harold observing Joey making a metal capsule.

"Do you think he might have hidden jewels or big bills in it?" Ethyl asked.

"Yes, and Harold thinks so too, but Detective Warren didn't mention anything about it when he interviewed me."

"You were interviewed by the police?" Ethyl looked impressed rather than repulsed by my revelation.

"Apparently, I'm on his list of suspects—if or when they determine that Joey was murdered."

Ethyl set her soda can on the end table. "Why?"

"My question exactly."

I told her about the Manor residents and others who had suggested Warren speak with me.

"No wonder I keep hearing your name bandied about. What possible motive could you have?" asked Ethyl.

"None. Certainly nothing compared to many other people in Russo's life."

Ethyl leaned forward and narrowed her eyes. "Let's brainstorm about where Russo could have put a capsule. Maybe no one's found it yet."

"You think while I make tea. Want some?"

"No thanks. I'll stick with soda."

I filled my electric kettle and put a tea bag in my cup. When the water started to gurgle, I poured it in.

"Come up with anything?" I asked Ethyl when I sat back down.

"I'm drawing a blank. You?"

I hated to admit it, but I was rather enjoying Ethyl's unplanned visit. And, as Harold always said, two heads were better than one.

I took a sip of my tea. "My first thought is the toilet tank."

Ethyl nodded. "That seems obvious but if the detective…what's his name?"

"Detective Warren."

"If Detective Warren didn't know about a possible stash, maybe he didn't look." Ethyl moved to the edge of her seat. "So how do we get into Joey's apartment to check?"

"There's no 'we' in this. Illegally entering his apartment could get YOU in big trouble. I wouldn't chance it," I warned.

"Well," Ethyl sipped her soda, "all Joey got for illegally entering YOUR apartment was a slap on the wrist."

"And dead," I reminded her.

"But his death is completely unrelated to him breaking into your apartment and setting off the fire alarms." She looked at me closely. "Isn't it?"

"I believe so, but you never know."

She sat back on the couch as if she'd already come up with an idea. "Nothing ventured, nothing gained. Isn't that what they say?"

"That's a 'dadism' for sure."

"A what?"

"Never mind. What's your plan?" I asked.

Ethyl scrunched up her forehead. "Since you're under investigation, wouldn't you rather not know?"

"I guess so. But…" I gave Ethyl a stern look, "If you do find a stash by whatever means, I suggest you leave it where you find it and send an anonymous tip to the police. Be careful, Ethyl. Detective Warren finds us old ladies to be easy marks."

"Thanks for the heads up." Ethyl slowly rose from the couch, no doubt stiff from sitting too long. "I'll keep in touch."

"Me too," I said as she left my apartment.

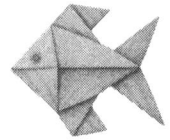

Chapter Seventeen

As I was getting ready for dinner, I had a text from Gloria.

> Rosa wants to know if you'd like to join us for a celebration dinner.

I didn't want to celebrate Russo's death if that's what she meant, but I did want to connect with the ladies, so I answered in the affirmative. I enjoyed their company and maybe Rosa had a lead on what happened to Joey.

> Let's go to Sam's Place this time. Something different, and there's less noise, so we can talk.

> Sounds good. We'll pick you up tomorrow at 6:00.

I gave her a thumbs-up emoji.

—

Later, Harold greeted me when he picked me up but we walked to dinner in silence. After we placed our orders—roast beef for him, chicken piccata for me—I asked, "What's up? You're unusually quiet tonight."

After fidgeting with his napkin, he looked over at me. "Agatha was standing outside the shop today when I left. She introduced herself, then proceeded to walk with me." Harold took a sip of his wine. "I didn't invite her; she just tagged along."

I must admit, as I visualized this encounter, I felt a pang of jealousy.

"She started asking me questions about Joey. If we were friends? Did we work on projects together? Had I been to his apartment recently?"

Our dinners arrived but I had lost my appetite. "Go on."

Harold bandied his knife around like he was about to slay a dragon. I chuckled when I remembered Ethyl referring to Agatha as The Dragon Lady.

"What's so funny?" Harold wanted to know.

"Nothing. What did you tell her?"

"The truth—we weren't friends, just acquaintances. No, I hadn't been to his apartment, and no, we didn't work on projects together. When she asked, I told her I didn't know what he was working on." Harold chewed a bite of meat. "She narrowed her eyes like she didn't believe me, then she took my arm."

"She took your arm?" I asked, louder than I meant to sound. I was being so uncool, but I couldn't help it. Harold didn't seem to notice. He was in defensive mode.

"I sped up so she had to let go. It didn't deter her, though. She continued to walk behind me, then followed me into the elevator where she got all flirty and reworded her questions. She probably thought I'd give in to her charms and give her different answers."

"Did you?"

"Of course not!"

"Well, she IS beautiful…especially by Manor standards."

Harold looked hurt. "Do you really think I'm that easily swayed? Actually, I felt insulted that she thought she could charm me into something."

I reached over and took Harold's hand. "I'm sorry. I know you're a man of principle and not easily manipulated by a pretty woman or anyone else, for that matter. It's just that this whole Russo and Agatha thing is making me edgy."

Looking around to see if anyone was listening, I whispered, "Ethyl thinks she's here to find the stash."

"You had another visit from Ethyl?" Harold asked.

"Yes, but it was friendly. She's really sharp when it comes to investigating."

I told Harold about Ethyl's observations concerning everything being fake when it came to Agatha.

He considered my statement for a moment. "I think she's right. When she took my arm, I didn't feel any tremor, and when I sped up, her uneven walk suddenly improved."

"So do you think Russo stashed the loot in the capsule, then put the capsule in the toilet tank?" I said under my breath.

"Let's talk about it later."

I knew Harold wanted to digest this new information, so I changed the subject. "I'm going to Sam's Place tomorrow night with Rosa and Gloria."

Harold's bushy brows shot up. "Why?"

"Why not? They're young and fun, and it's a way to get out of this place for the evening. Besides," I gave Harold a little nudge with my foot, "the danger from Russo is past."

"Don't be lulled into complacency, my dear. There could be a killer on the loose, and no one knows who their next victim might be."

Although my one glass of beer had gone to my head, Harold's comment sobered me up. "As usual, you're thinking about this situation with a clearer head than mine." I put my hand on my heart. "I'll be careful. I promise."

We were quiet while we concentrated on eating. "Want to help me do some research?" I asked Harold when we'd finished.

He scrunched up his forehead and cocked his head to the side. "Related to what?"

"You'll see. Let's go to my place."

Harold got up from the table. "You're going to do this research whether I'm there or not, so I might as well be there." He came around and pulled out my chair. "Ready, Freddie?"

I got up and possessively took Harold's arm. He seemed a little surprised but went with it. "Yep!"

"You go put your soft clothes on. I'll fire up your computer," Harold said after we entered my apartment.

When I returned to the living room, Harold was sitting in front of my Mac. "I assume you're wanting to Google something. What is it?"

I pulled a chair over and sat next to him. "Ask it to tell us what smells like bitter almonds."

Harold dutifully typed in the words without asking any questions.

"Well?" I asked when I saw that something had popped up.

Harold read aloud. "It says, Hydrogen cyanide or HCN, and benzaldehyde are chemicals that smell like bitter almonds."

"Anything else?"

"Only half the population is capable of detecting the smell of cyanide." Harold looked over at me. "Is Ethyl one of the fifty percent?"

"It seems so. The afternoon she came to my apartment after Russo was found dead, she said an EMT and then a policeman smelled the spilled liquid. When I asked her if she smelled anything in the room she said, 'bitter almonds,' thinking it was some kind of room freshener. It obviously wasn't."

Harold got up and moved to the couch. "Good detective work! Seems like you've sniffed out a partner with a nose as good as yours."

I joined Harold and took his hand. This Agatha thing was giving me a new perspective. He, on the other hand, was still focused on the Joey Case.

"So, the premise is that Russo was poisoned with cyanide hidden in a glass of red juice or wine. Right?"

"Seems like it. What do you think?" I asked. Harold always had good ideas.

"Have you thought about suicide? Maybe he was more depressed than I thought."

I went to get a drink of water. All this talk of poison was making me thirsty. "The possibility crossed my mind, but it's hard to dismiss the fact that he had several enemies."

I returned to the couch and took a sip. "I'm wondering about the stash—assuming there was one. Do you think the killer took it? Did the would-be killer toss Joey's apartment earlier?"

Harold got up and walked to the door. "I don't have the answers, but if Agatha's actions tell us anything, my guess is that no one's found anything yet." Harold opened the door, then leaned over and kissed me on the cheek. "You be careful, Martha. My gut tells me this whole thing isn't over yet."

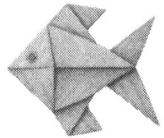

Chapter Eighteen

Gloria and Rosa were casually dressed in ripped jeans and t-shirts. They probably looked up Sam's Place and discovered it was a neighborhood bar. After ordering our usual burgers and beers, they asked if I'd heard any details regarding Joey's death.

I debated about how much to say, but I figured I needed to give them something if I expected them to participate in my investigation. "I don't think he died of natural causes; it was either murder or suicide, and cyanide was involved."

"WHAT?" they said in unison, drawing the attention of the patrons nearby.

I put my fingers on my lips.

"How do you know it was cyanide?" Rosa asked, using her inside voice.

"I can't reveal my source, but I'll bet in a week or two the police will come out with poison being the cause of death."

"Well, what do you know," Rosa said, then took a sip of her beer. The place was fairly quiet, and we'd been served right away. "Anything else?"

I decided to take a chance. "Changing the subject, do either of you know a red-headed woman named Agatha? She's quite lovely."

Rosa's eyes grew hard, and she leaned into the table. "Agatha Esposito?"

"I don't remember her last name. Describe her."

Rosa pursed her lips. "She's about my age, tall, red hair, fake boobs, and mean as hell."

"How do you know her?" I asked, thinking that I finally had something to tell Ethyl.

"She had an affair with my husband," Rosa snarled.

Even though her voice was even and low, Rosa's face was red, and I didn't think it was from the beer.

"Joey?" I asked.

"Who else?"

Gloria looked at Rosa. "You never said anything about an Agatha."

Rosa took a big gulp of her beer. "The subject was too embarrassing to talk about. It's not exactly flattering to be displaced by someone like HER."

"When did this happen?" Gloria asked.

"After we moved here, Joey was real restless, like. Bored. Probably depressed. I suggested he join the local gym and he did. All of a sudden, he was gone every afternoon. 'I'm goin' to the gym,' he'd say. He'd return home rumpled but not sweaty, and when there was no change in his paunch, I started getting suspicious."

Our dinners arrived and Rosa squeezed a pool of Ketchup onto her plate.

Gloria ignored her burger. "So?"

"So, one day I made a visit to the gym." Rosa took a bite of her burger.

"And no Joey?" Gloria prompted.

Rosa paused to chew. "No Joey. When I asked the manager about him, SHE spilled the beans."

I smiled. "Ahh, a woman manager."

"Yep. Otherwise, I don't think I would have gotten a damn thing. Anyway, she said Joey had become friends with a red-headed woman, and on most days they left the gym together all cozy like."

Gloria wanted details. "So, what did you do?"

"I confronted the bastard. He hemmed and hawed, then finally admitted to having the affair. This wasn't the first time, so it was the last straw for me. I kicked him out of the house and started divorce proceedings."

I'd been patient, but I couldn't hold out any longer. "Do you think Agatha killed Joey? And if so, what was her motive?"

Rosa didn't answer right away and I gave my head a little shake when I saw Gloria about to push her into speaking.

"Maybe," Rosa finally said. "I think she'd do anything to get her way. When I confronted her about Joey, she told me to stay out of her business or she'd have her brothers pay me a visit."

"Sounds like a threat," I said.

"That's what I thought. Don't it make you wonder why a woman that beautiful would have anything to do with Joey? I think she knows about the potential stash from the heist and wants to get her grubby hands on it." Rosa sat back in the booth.

"Have you met Ralph Jensen?" I asked.

Rosa picked up a French fry and dipped it in Ketchup. "Name sounds familiar. How do you know him?"

"He was a friend of Joey's and I ran into him at the Manor a while back. He said he was visiting. Big guy, shaggy hair and beard, construction worker clothes, and boots. Not at all friendly. Sound familiar?"

Rosa cocked her head to the side. "Sounds like someone from the old neighborhood. Joey had several friends who could fit that description. Did he have a Brooklyn accent?"

With the guy towering over me, I hadn't noticed his accent. "He might have. About all he said was 'get out of my way.' I wouldn't let him pass until he told me his name. I never did find out how he got into the building, but I'm sure he was a friend of Joey's."

Gloria held out her hand. Bending one finger down, she started counting off suspects. "So, we have this Ralph guy and Agatha—who else is a suspect?"

"JR." I said.

"Junior?" Rosa asked. "Good grief, Martha, you know him, too?"

I nodded. "I also ran into him at the Manor. I knew him right away because he looked just like his dad. At least he was cordial. Said he was there because of 'unfinished business'."

"And just who is JR?" Gloria asked.

"My late," Rosa smiled at the word, "husband's son by a previous marriage."

Gloria put one more finger down. "Anybody else? Is there anyone at the Manor besides you," she looked at me, "who wanted to see him bumped off?"

"Me?" I asked a little too loudly. "I never said I wanted Joey bumped off. I said I wanted him out of the Manor. I hope neither of you told the police that I wanted him dead." I gave each lady a serious look.

Both put their palms up. "The police haven't talked to me," Gloria said. "Why would they?"

"They paid me a visit," Rosa admitted. "They wanted to know about the altercation in the Manor's dining room and if I thought you had anything to do with Joey's death. I told them that Joey had interrupted our lunch, and I was sure you had nothing to do with him showing up dead."

"Anything else?" I asked, feeling that there was more to the story.

"They wanted to know where I was the day he was found, and I told them I was in my condo watching television by myself," Rosa answered in a confident voice. She was still on my suspect's list, but barely. My intuition was telling me she probably didn't kill her ex.

The waitress brought our check. I was running out of time, so I asked a final question. "Assuming Joey was murdered, who do you think did it?" I directed my question to Rosa.

She reached for the check this time. "I wish I knew. I'd send them a thank you card," she said with some venom in her voice.

I took my last sip of beer. "The only way I'm going to get off Detective Warren's suspect list is to figure out who did this, assuming they decide that Joey was murdered. Warren's not the best cop in the world, and I'm easy prey so, if you come up with any ideas or hear news from the old neighborhood, I'd appreciate it if you let me know."

Rosa looked genuinely concerned. "I'm sorry you had to get mixed up in all this Joey shit. Even back in the day, he was the rotten apple at the bottom of the barrel who made the good apples around him smell bad."

"We're your friends, Martha. If we hear anything from the old neighborhood, you'll be the first to know," Gloria assured me. Rosa nodded her agreement.

Chapter Nineteen

After I was safely back in my apartment, I texted Harold.

> I'm back. Guess what?

Good. What?

> Agatha had an affair with Joey when he was married to Rosa!

That's an interesting tidbit. Save the rest for tomorrow. Good night, Martha. 🖤

> Good night.

I saw Ethyl at lunch and asked if I could join her. Laura wasn't feeling well and was eating lunch in her apartment. When a smile lit up Ethyl's face, I sat down and then gave her the news about Agatha's affair.

"Well, well," she said. "So does that move the ex-wife to the top of the suspects list?"

"I don't think so. My instincts are telling me Rosa didn't do it, even though she has a motive," I replied, wondering if my friendship with the woman was clouding my better judgment.

We both raised the possibility of Agatha being the perpetrator, but we couldn't come up with a motive other than the possible stash.

After lunch, I took the minivan to my hair salon. Two ladies joined me in the van, whispering between themselves. I ignored them.

My stylist took one look at me and asked, "What's going on, Martha?"

Kathleen had been cutting and coloring my hair since I moved to Poughkeepsie, and we'd become friends. Stylists are like bartenders and therapists. People share things with them that they wouldn't ordinarily share with others. Over the years, Kathleen had learned to immediately tap into the demeanor of her clients and know if something was off with them. She was an exceptionally intuitive person.

Green and purple crystals were lined up on her station's counter along with a plaque that read:

LORD, KEEP YOUR ARM AROUND MY SHOULDER
AND YOUR HAND OVER MY MOUTH.

She had curly red hair, mischievous brown eyes, and a "throw it at me, I won't flinch" kind of personality.

When I told her I was a suspect in a murder investigation, she asked for the particulars. "Not many details," I replied. "The police aren't sure whether it was murder or suicide." I leaned in and whispered, "I think it was cyanide that killed him."

Kathleen raised her eyebrows but said nothing in response. She'd heard it all. "Any suspects you could steer my way?" she asked with a smirk. "I'm an expert when it comes to wheedling out confessions and confidential information."

Agatha immediately popped into my head. She'd have to get that red hair touched up somewhere. "There is a redhead…"

Kathleen perked up and pointed to her own hair. "This color?"

"A little brighter but similar."

"Send her in. I'll have her telling me her secrets in no time."

I shook my head. "It's not that easy. We aren't friends. In fact, she's after Harold."

"Harold?" Kathleen shout whispered.

"About ten minutes into our first meeting, she asked me if we were sleeping together. Later, she sidled up to him, thinking her charms would win him over."

"Did it work?"

"No!" I might have said that a bit too emphatically. "He was on to her right away. He thinks she's looking for intel about the deceased."

Kathleen finished globbing on color solution and ushered me to another chair to process. "You mean the Joey-guy."

"Yes."

Kathleen motioned to her next client to take a seat in her chair. "Hold that thought, Martha. I'll get back to you in twenty minutes."

"Go on," Kathleen said after she'd rinsed off the excess color and had me back in her chair for a trim.

"She thinks Harold might know where Joey hid some valuables."

Holding the scissors in midair, Kathleen said, "Hmmm, after my ex died, we looked all over for any kind of stash. He was a Joe, too. They could have been buddies."

"Did you find anything?"

"Yes. We found some cash and jewelry in an air vent."

After a brief blow-dry, I paid Kathleen and made my next appointment. "I'll see what I can do about getting the redhead in here before my next visit. Ethyl might get her to come."

"Ethyl? I thought she was your archenemy."

"She was, but now she isn't. A story for next month. See you then."

—

The next day, I waylaid Ethyl in the hall and asked her about getting Agatha to have Kathleen color her hair. "I'll see what I can do. She seems like the type who might do her own," Ethyl said when I handed her Kathleen's business card.

"Let me know if you're successful. I want to give Kathleen a heads up."

—

My son called the following morning. "Is it April already?" I asked. I could tell from the silence at the other end that Richard was worried about my memory. "I'm just kidding. I know that tomorrow is April first. Are you going to April Fool me?"

More silence. "Never mind. I'll see you tomorrow at noon."

"Have a good day, Mother."

—

The cafeteria was all abuzz at breakfast. As soon as I sat down, Ethyl descended on me like a bat out of hell with a newspaper in her hand.

"Have you seen this?" she breathlessly asked, holding the paper in front of my face.

When I took the paper, a headline jumped out at me.

An Arrest Has Been Made In
A Possible Murder At Martyn Manor

I looked over at Ethyl, who was making pushing motions with her hands. "Read the article!"

I quickly scanned the half-page spread. Basically, it said that a Ms. Agatha Esposito, temporary resident at Martyn Manor, had been arrested as a suspect in the death of Mr. Joey Russo after she was caught breaking into his apartment.

Other than, "Good grief!" I was speechless.

"Now isn't that something?" Ethyl said, taking back her paper.

"That's something all right. Do you think she did it?" I asked.

"Killed him, you mean? I don't know but…" Ethyl leaned across the table and whispered, "I think she did what I was going to do, got caught doing it, and now they think she did the deed."

It took me a minute to put this word puzzle together. "Good thing you held off. It could be your name splashed across page two."

"I know," Ethyl said with some alarm in her voice.

"So, the breaking and entering was all it took to arrest her on suspicion of murder?"

"That and the fact she lied about absolutely everything on her application to this place."

"How do you know that?" I asked.

Ethyl smiled, "I have my sources."

"I thought we were partners."

"I'll explain later." She looked around at the crowded dining room. "Not here."

—

After a good workout and a change of clothes, I settled myself at my usual table for lunch. When I saw Richard purposefully striding through the door with a newspaper in his hand, I knew right away what our conversation was going to be about. He placed the paper on the table, greeted me, then headed to the cafeteria line. When he returned with a burger and fries on his tray, I knew there was going to be trouble. This was stress-eating for Richard.

Before he could say anything, I preempted the conversation. "I've read the article."

Richard looked slightly disappointed that he wasn't bringing me the news. "This is, or was, Gloria's friend, Rosa's, ex-husband!"

"You're correct," I said.

"Do you know this Agatha person?"

"Yes, we've met, but we definitely aren't friends. However, I'm not convinced she murdered Mr. Russo. In fact, I'm not convinced he was murdered at all."

My son had his lawyer face on. He was all business. "So, what do you believe was his cause of death?"

"I think he died from cyanide poisoning, but it could have been a suicide. He was depressed and, basically, friendless. He wasn't a nice man."

Richard looked at me like I'd just jumped out of a cake. "You seem to know a lot about this Russo person and the investigation into his death."

I shrugged. "I live under the same roof he did. It's a small world."

The burger looked delicious. Not as greasy as Sam's Place, but good. I wondered why I never ordered a burger for lunch.

"Mother, are you listening?"

"I'm sorry, what did you say?"

"I don't think it's safe for you to live here any longer." Richard ticked off the reasons on his fingers. "There were the false fire alarms, the purse snatcher, the director being fired for theft, and now this. I'll start looking around right away for a new living arrangement for you."

I held up my hand. "Hold on, Richard. Don't I have a say in where I live?"

"Of course, but you certainly don't want to live in a community that's dangerous, do you?"

Alarm bells were going off in my head, but I knew I had to remain calm and reasonable, even though I felt like shouting, "I won't move! You can't make me!" The truth was, maybe he could.

I slowly set my turkey wrap on the plate. "I understand that Mr. Russo's death was a dramatic event. Even alarming, I suppose. However, I feel perfectly safe here. Joey, ahh, Mr. Russo, was a gangster type from Brooklyn. He had enemies. He wasn't in good health and he was depressed. I'm none of those things."

When Richard didn't respond, I continued. "This is my home. I have friends here, I have a life here. I'm too old to start over. Please don't consider moving me." I hadn't meant to, but when I teared up, my son softened his tone.

"I understand, Mother, but I'd never forgive myself if you were caught up in something nefarious here."

I patted his hand. "Don't worry. I mind my own business and have reliable friends like Harold. You trust Harold to watch out for me, don't you?"

"Yes, I trust Harold implicitly. But…"

"Let's just close the book on this discussion for now. We can circle back later." I pointed to his half-eaten burger. "Finish your lunch. It's getting cold."

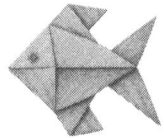

Chapter Twenty

When Harold and I returned to my apartment following dinner that night, I told him about Richard wanting to move me to another facility. Before I expressed my opinion, I asked him for his. I wanted to get a man's perspective, and I respected Harold's logical thinking.

Harold was quiet for a long time then he cleared his throat, which indicated he was about to say something significant. "I've been thinking about this for a while."

"You have?"

"Don't interrupt, Martha."

"Sorry."

"I think you should ask your son to terminate his contract on your apartment."

I must have given a little gasp because Harold looked at me before continuing. "Then, if you're financially able, I think you should rent the studio apartment next door to me. It's available. We'll have maintenance cut a door between your place and mine. The studio will be your bedroom, bathroom, and study. We can share the living room in my place. This arrangement will give you complete independence to make your own decisions. You'll no longer have to fear what your son might do in the future."

When I began to speak, Harold held up his hand. "I'm not quite done. I know your son is concerned about your safety, as am I, but I think you'd get yourself into the mix wherever you lived. At least here, I can keep an eye on you. Besides…" Harold leaned toward me and added in a husky voice, "I can't imagine life here without you."

"I think…"

"One last thing," Harold interjected. "When you move to the studio," he looked hopeful, "IF you move to the studio, I think we should get married."

Harold ignored my gasp, which was louder this time, and kept talking. "Then should I die before you, you'll get my Survivor Benefits from the government. No sense in having them go to waste." He sat back, apparently satisfied with speaking his peace. "What do you say?"

As shocked as I was at his proposals, I heard myself speaking calmly. "You've obviously been thinking about this for a while."

"I have."

I took a big breath. "That's a lot to take in all at once."

"Just think about it, Martha. It's a logical plan. Besides," Harold put his hand over his heart, "I really would like to marry you if you'll have me. Our lives wouldn't change much; you'd still have your own space, and I'd have mine. Call me crazy, but I'd like to be your husband and not just your boyfriend or whatever it is you call me."

I closed my eyes and tried to imagine being someone's wife…again. "Aren't we too old for all this?"

"All what?"

"Getting married. We already live under the same roof and spend most evenings together." When Harold remained quiet—he also knew the power of silence—I started saying out loud what was flowing through my mind. "I would like to be independent from my son. I appreciate his generosity and caring, but I've always owned or co-owned my home. Before now, I never took a penny from my parents or anyone else, for that matter. Richard whisked me away so fast I didn't have time to think it through and then, boom, here I was dependent on him, which gives him some power over my destiny."

I paused for a breath then continued with my unfiltered train of thought. "What if he remarries and moves away? What if he insists that I move to a new location? I've always been an independent woman. I don't know how I got myself into this bind."

Harold wasn't getting sucked into my emotional diatribe. He remained logical. "Can you afford the studio? I know it's a personal question but we…" he fiddled with the clasp on his jumpsuit, "we may be headed into new territory on several levels. If we were to get married, I believe we each need to provide full financial disclosure. Don't you?"

"Absolutely, and, to answer your question, I believe I can afford the studio. My entrance fee is paid. I'll check on the studio rent and confirm that it's available."

When Harold smiled, I rushed on. "That doesn't mean I've made any decisions, but I am willing to at least get the facts before I do. Fair?"

"Fair."

Harold got up from the recliner, and I joined him at the door. "I love you, Martha. I'd be proud to have you as my wife."

I could feel a smile creeping across my face and warmth blooming in my cheeks. "I love you too, Harold. You've given me a lot to think about." I reached up and kissed him. "Good night, sleep tight."

He drew me into a tight hug. "And don't let the bedbugs bite," Harold whispered in my ear before walking out and closing the door.

After Harold left, I changed into my nightie and crawled into bed. "Alexa, play relaxing music," I commanded. I put two pillows behind me and leaned against the headboard, my mind swirling with possibilities.

I said I'd never marry again and here I was contemplating Harold's proposal. Living in the same space did make sense, considering we spent every evening together, but what if Harold ended up in skilled care? Would I be stuck living in a studio apartment for my final years? Would the government benefits allow me to take over the larger apartment if he died?

I closed my eyes and concentrated on a Brahms lullaby but my mind soon came back online. On the other hand, what if my son terminated his arrangement with the Manor, and I was suddenly forced to move? What if this murder thing blew over, but Richard relocated to Timbuktu next year and insisted I follow him?

The lullaby ended, and a Beethoven piece came on that I recognized but couldn't name. My mind bloomed with details. I could move my recliner to Harold's apartment so we'd both be comfortable in his living room. My dinette table would fit in the studio and serve as a workspace. We could use Harold's table for take-in dining or playing games. We have our separate activities so we wouldn't be in each other's way during the day.

There was a lot to consider on the financial side. Before I could make a decision about moving to a studio, I'd need to talk to the admissions people. Was it really possible to put a door between the two apartments? Would Harold want to get married even if I didn't move? I moved the extra pillow aside and asked Alexa to turn off the music, hoping to have more clarity in the morning.

Feeling a combination of excitement and anxiety, it took a while for my brain to turn off so I could sleep.

—

My cell phone rang just as I was about to leave for breakfast.
Hello.
Yes, I'll be here this afternoon. What time?
All right.
I texted Harold.

> Detective Warren is returning for more questions this afternoon. Can you come to my place about 2:00?

> Of course. See you then.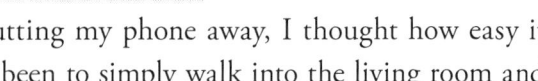

After putting my phone away, I thought how easy it would have been to simply walk into the living room and tell Harold about the call instead of texting.

Chapter Twenty-One

It was full-on Spring in Poughkeepsie but I felt chilled. Maybe it was the weather, cloudy with intermittent rain and a blustery wind rattling the windows, reminding me of the night someone entered my apartment. Maybe it was the scheduled visit from Detective Warren, always a chilling experience. Whenever I was interviewed, I felt I had to be on my toes every moment, carefully considering the answers to each question he asked.

Ethyl was in the hall when I came out of my apartment to go to breakfast.

"I have a little news," she said. It was good to see Ethyl smiling. I was still testing out this newfound relationship but so far, Ethyl had stayed on course of being more friend than foe.

"Good. I need something to distract me."

"Want to say more?"

"Nope. Tell me your news."

We got on the elevator. "Just before she got arrested, I gave Agatha the business card for your hairdresser. You might want to check with…what's her name?"

"Kathleen."

"You might want to check with Kathleen and see if Dragon Lady has an appointment yet. I heard she's out on bail and living in an apartment somewhere here in town."

We stepped out of the elevator and into the dining room. "That's not much news but maybe Kathleen will have something. I'll call her today."

We went through the line and sat together at a nearby table. Rain slashed against the windows and the lights flickered.

"Some storm," Ethyl said, stirring cream into her coffee. "I'd hate to be out in this."

"Maybe it will keep Detective Warren away."

"Away from where?"

"From here. He's coming to ask me more questions."

To her credit, Ethyl looked alarmed. "That's not fair! If anything, he should be questioning me again. After all, I was there when Jimmy discovered Russo's body." Ethyl set her spoon down and looked into my eyes. "I told him in no uncertain terms that you were nowhere in the vicinity of Russo's apartment. Do you think he's determined to pin this on you?"

"I don't know. I think he's mad that I solved a few cases around here and made him look bad."

"When's he coming?"

"This afternoon."

"Want me to be with you?"

"Thanks for the offer, but Harold said he'd come over. He knows how to handle Warren and I think having a man present helps to keep the detective in line."

Ethyl nodded. "Just know I'm here for you if you need me."

What a transformation! Ethyl The Terrible to Ethyl The Friend.

—

The rain had let up some by the time Warren walked through my door with a dripping trench coat laid across his arm.

He opened with, "No matter where this investigation takes us, your name pops up, Mrs. Anderson. Want to comment on that?"

I was sitting on the couch and Harold was on the recliner, so Warren pulled up a dinette chair. In addition to his still-rumpled suit, I noticed that his wet shoes were worn down at the heel, the laces frayed. I answered. "Not unless you have a specific question."

Harold gave me a barely perceptible nod of approval.

"Every suspect on our list has a link to you." Warren ticked the names off. "Rosa Russo, Ethyl Haggerty, JR Russo, Ralph Jensen, Agatha Esposito. When asked, each one said they knew you. Care to elaborate?"

"It's true. I have met each person you just named. After all, as I've told you before, I'm an official ambassador for the Manor. It's my job to meet new people."

Warren scowled. "But Rosa, JR, and Ralph aren't residents."

I skooched to the front of the couch cushion. "No, but they've all been here, have they not?"

Warren ignored my question. "On the day of Mr. Russo's untimely death, Ethyl Haggerty's fingerprints were found all over his apartment. In fact, SHE was in the apartment when the paramedics showed up. Do you know why she happened to be there?"

"She told me that she was walking by his apartment, found the door partially open, and the orderly kneeling over a body. When he realized that Mr. Russo was dead, Jimmy became distressed, so Ethyl offered him a glass of water and stayed with him until other employees and the EMTs arrived."

Warren took notes, never looking up as I spoke. I wondered if he was avoiding eye contact for some reason.

"And Agatha Esposito? Why do you think she broke into Russo's apartment?"

I looked over at Harold and he verbally stepped forward to answer the question. "It's been rumored that Joey had some cash or valuables stashed away. Since Agatha has a history with Joey, we're," Harold looked at me, "assuming she was looking for the stash."

Warren looked at me for confirmation and I pointed to Harold. "What he said."

"Any ideas about JR and Jensen?" Warren's pen was poised over the notepad. Apparently, his memory was about as good as mine.

"As you know, JR is Joey's son and Jensen was an old friend. They were here to visit him. That's all I know." I sat back in the cushions. What an exhausting exercise. "Anything else, Detective?"

"One more thing. I've learned that you're a friend of Mr. Russo's ex-wife. Is that true?"

"Yes, Rosa and I are friends."

"In your capacity of ambassador," Warren said the word with some disdain, "have you ever seen her lurking in the halls?"

"To my knowledge, she has only been in the dining room. She was my guest for lunch, along with our mutual friend, Gloria. It was the day Russo had to be removed from the vicinity of our table. Remember?"

"She has never been to your apartment or to Mr. Russo's apartment?"

"She has never been in my apartment, and I doubt if she was ever in Joey's. However, I can't confirm that." I decided to try something I'd seen on TV shows. "I heard that the only prints on the glass were those of the deceased. Is that true?"

Warren didn't answer, but his body language said it all, and I believed my intuition was right on the money. I had no idea about prints on the glass, but it was a good guess, leading me to believe more strongly in the possibility that Joey had offed himself using the drama of cyanide. It fit with a guy who would illegally enter an apartment and steal a can of soda. Even in his death, he wanted to stir up trouble by casting a shadow of suspicion over his enemies.

Harold spoke using his military voice. "Are we done here, Detective? I believe you've more than thoroughly questioned Martha. She had absolutely nothing to do with the death of Joey Russo. In fact, I believe that additional questioning could be considered harassment."

Warren gave Harold a sharp look. "What do you know about this supposed stash? Did Russo confide in you about it?"

"As I told you earlier, I know nothing and Joey didn't confide in me," Harold said. "All I know is he was making some kind of metal container. He never told me what it was for. Although I frequently saw him in the workshop, we spoke very little. Anything else?"

Warren closed his book with a clap, grabbed his coat off the back of the chair, and stood up. He pointed at me. "I'm going to solve this case without your help." When I started to get up, he added with a grunt, "I'll see myself out."

"Is it my imagination, or do you think Warren's trying to pin a murder on me?" I asked Harold after Warren was safely down the hall.

"You certainly seem to be a burr in his side. Great tactic asking him about the glass. You had no idea whether or not there were additional prints, did you?"

"Nope. But I read him like a book."

"Me too, which is making me think more and more that this could have been a suicide."

"Makes sense."

Harold got up to leave, then turned back. "Any thoughts on what we talked about last night?"

"Not yet. I'm still thinking." I poked Harold with my elbow. "My brain's old and slow."

He kissed me on the cheek. "No pressure. Just checking."

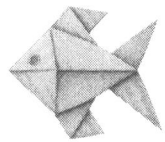

Chapter Twenty-Two

It was Wednesday and I had chair yoga in the afternoon so I texted Kathleen right after breakfast, asking her to contact me when she had a break.

It was just before lunch and I was embroidering when my phone pinged. It was a text from Kathleen.

> Agatha Esposito has an appointment with me tomorrow!

Great! If you can, find out why she was renting at the Manor, why she illegally entered Joey's apartment, and if she thinks he was murdered.

> That's a tall order. I'll do what I can.

I sent Kathleen thumbs up emoji and a pink heart. Next, I texted Laura to inquire about her health.

> I'm good. Pick me up for lunch?

After thinking a minute about Ethyl, I texted Laura back.

Would you mind if Ethyl joined us? She's been doing some good investigative work. We could bring you up to date.

Next, I texted Ethyl.

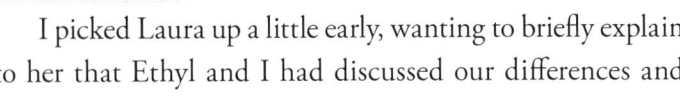

I'll be there. 🖤

I picked Laura up a little early, wanting to briefly explain to her that Ethyl and I had discussed our differences and become tentative friends.

"That was a big departure. Sworn enemy to friend," Laura said as we got off the elevator.

"I know. I still consider the friendship probationary. The change in Ethyl was swift, and I want to see if it lasts. I hope you don't mind her eating with us. She, too, is looking for friends and something interesting to do," I lowered my voice, "like investigate the death of Joey Russo."

Laura chuckled. "I've missed this."

Ethyl was already in the cafeteria when we entered. After selecting our food, we joined her.

I opened with, "Agatha has an appointment with Kathleen tomorrow."

"Really?" Ethyl asked.

We filled Laura in on the basics concerning Agatha and our high hopes of getting information about her intentions via Kathleen.

"What else is new?" Laura asked.

"Detective Warren came to visit me again. It was my third interview. Very unpleasant, and there seemed to be something off with him. He looked like he'd slept in his clothes and he had dark circles under his eyes. He was even more accusatory than usual. I hope someone comes up with the cause of Joey's death soon."

Laura looked at Ethyl, then at me. "What's your gut telling you?"

Ethyl spoke up first. "I think Agatha paid Joey a little evening visit," she tipped her head to one side, "if you know what I mean." When we both nodded, she continued. "While she was there, she planned to locate the stash, but the only time she was out of Joey's sight was when she went to the bathroom. When she found nothing there, she decided to put cyanide in his cranberry juice then have another go at his apartment later—when he was no longer around. If you know what I mean."

"She just happened to have cyanide crystals in her purse?" Laura asked.

"How she happened to have cyanide is the $64,000 question. You're an author, do you have any ideas? Have you ever killed off a character using cyanide?" Ethyl asked.

Laura took a sip of her coffee. She had a sly smile on her face. "Not recently, but I have researched the subject. After all, Agatha Christie frequently did her victims in with poisons, and cyanide was one of her favorites."

"Do you think Agatha studied Agatha to figure out how to knock Joey off? Now wouldn't that be something?" I couldn't help myself.

We all chucked then Laura continued. "Other authors have also used cyanide. Ever heard of Isaac Asimov's *Whiff of Death* or William Kuienzle's *Sudden Death*? They used cyanide." Laura looked at us, obviously pleased to be a contributing member of the team.

"Wow," Ethyl blurted. When other diners looked over, she said more quietly, "You're like a walking encyclopedia of information about…you know," she lowered her voice to a whisper, "poisons."

I needed to wrap up our luncheon discussion because I'd promised to meet a new move-in at Bingo. "Let's reconvene on Friday after I talk to Kathleen tomorrow afternoon."

"Does this mean we're not having lunch together tomorrow?" Ethyl asked in a sheepish voice.

Laura spoke up. "Of course not. There's no reason we can't eat together every day…case or not."

"I agree. In the meantime, I'll research how someone might get their hands on cyanide. I doubt if it's something you just order on Amazon," I offered.

We three left the table together. I felt like I was part of the Three Musketeers who, if I was remembering correctly, were united by a strong bond of brotherhood. Their motto, "all for one and one for all," reflected their commitment to each other and their shared ideals.

—

Sue Dalton, the new move-in, was waiting outside the activity room door when I arrived. Bingo wasn't an ideal environment in which to get to know someone, so we stayed after the others left.

About my age, Sue was on the tall side, had the usual white hair, a serious personality, but mischievous blue eyes. She seemed to have difficulty catching her breath after speaking, which made me wonder what brought her to the Manor.

"Tell me about yourself," I said. We'd dispensed with the usual chit chat during Bingo.

"I was a librarian. Research was my specialty." Sue took a deep breath. "Doctoral candidates at the University of Missouri frequently came to me for help. Of course, much of that changed with the advent of Google and AI, but I'm still a researcher at heart."

I liked Sue and decided to take a chance on her fitting in with The Three Musketeers. I figured we could become the Four Horsewomen, not harbingers of end times exactly, but powerful.

"Can you research how someone might procure cyanide?"

Sue's eyes widened. "Did I hear you correctly? Cyanide? Whatever for?"

Since no one was in the room, I figured it was an ideal time to explain the Russo Case to her. I skipped the beginning about when I took him down and got him arrested, and started with his death and the various suspects in his possible murder, including myself. I emphasized Agatha Esposito as my personal favorite for the job. I also told her about my friend Ethyl smelling bitter almond shortly after discovering the body and our suspicion that cyanide was used, either by his own hand or the hand of another.

"Good heavens!"

"I know, it's a lot. What do you think?"

Without a minute of hesitation, Sue replied, "I'm in! I'll start right away on the research. I still have access to academic sites not accessible to the general public. When do you need the information?"

"ASAP. I'd like to get this monkey off my back. We'll know more about our primary suspect tomorrow after I speak with Kathleen. You can meet the rest of the team at lunch. We gather at 11:30. Laura is an author, Ethyl is a…" I paused, realizing I knew very little about Ethyl. "…a reformed scamp. I'll tell you more someday. And me," I pointed to myself, "I'm an old lady who likes to get into good trouble."

Sue stood to leave. "This was some meeting, Madame Ambassador." She did a little bow. "New friends and a new adventure await. I'm delighted to have made your acquaintance."

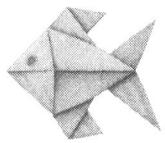

Chapter Twenty-Three

When I got back to my apartment, I fell into my recliner. Since I was so tired, I texted Harold to see if he'd bring take-out for our dinner.

> Sure. What do you want me to pick up?

I'm easy. You decide. See you about 5:30.

I had a lot to think about. I knew Harold was getting antsy waiting for my decision concerning moving and marriage. I didn't blame him, but these were life- altering commitments and I wasn't going to allow him to rush me. I did, however, pull myself together long enough to make an appointment to speak with someone at the admissions office in the morning.

—

Later that afternoon, my granddaughter, Barbara, called to ask about coming for a visit on Mother's Day weekend. She'd bring her wife, Bobbie, and baby Marti. They lived in Chicago, and I rarely saw them so of course, I said yes. Although it was weeks away, I made a note to myself to make room reservations and other plans before time got away from me.

I realized that the Russo Case was taking up too much space in my brain. With a limited capacity in the first place, it was challenging to consider so many things at one time.

"For Heaven's Sake, Martha. Get a grip," I said to myself before asking Alexa to play relaxing music. Since I wasn't going to dinner, I changed into my soft clothes. Taking my bra off and putting on a sweatshirt and old yoga pants felt delightful.

I was glad I'd suggested having dinner in my apartment because I could fill Harold in on the Russo Case, including telling him about Sue, our new researcher. I was confident that if anyone could find out about how to buy cyanide, she could.

—

Harold arrived with two to-go boxes. "Your choice," he opened the boxes and pointed. "Salisbury steak or chicken something-or-other."

"I'll take the chicken," I said as I cut the tops off the boxes to make them seem more plate-like.

Harold looked at me. "Tired, huh?"

"Yeah. It's been a busy day." When I saw the hopeful look in Harold's eyes, I gave him a crumb. "I'm meeting with someone in the admissions office tomorrow morning. I'll let you know what I find out about fees for a studio and if they'd be willing to cut out a door."

He noticeably brightened. "That's good news. What else you got?"

"I met a new move-in today, Sue Dalton. She's a retired librarian who has expertise in research. She's going to find out how a person can buy cyanide on the open market."

"Really?"

"Yep. I'm thinking either Agatha bought it and killed Joey with it, or she bought it for him to use on himself."

"Why Agatha?"

"Just a hunch. One way or the other, she was definitely here at the Manor because of Joey." I gave Harold a little kick under the table. "Besides wooing you, of course."

Harold got up, poured himself a glass of burgundy, then returned to the table. "You're probably right. About the Joey thing, I mean. What else?"

"My hairdresser, Kathleen, is doing Agatha's hair tomorrow so she'll get the scoop and pass it on to me."

Harold looked at me over his glass. "Isn't there some kind of confidentiality agreement between hairdressers and their clients?"

"Of course not."

Harold snickered.

"You were kidding, weren't you?"

"I was. I hope you know what you're doing, Martha." Harold gave me his serious look: narrowed eyes, firm mouth, slightly cocked head.

—

The next morning, I paid a visit to the admissions office. Jeff Somebody was the director. He told me that the studio next to Harold's apartment was still available, and it was possible to cut out a portion of the wall and install a door between the two apartments. When we went over the financials, I came away feeling confident that I could swing the monthly payments and become self-sufficient, although it would mean being careful with my discretionary funds going forward.

Heck, I only needed to stretch my funds for a few more years. I knew, however, if I ended up in memory care, my costs would go up substantially. I also wondered what my son would think about me declining his help. He might be relieved, given his new state as a single person, or he might be angry that I no longer wanted to accept his generosity. It was hard to know.

—

Upon arriving at the cafeteria for lunch, I was surprised to see Sue with an oxygen thingy in her nose. I introduced her to Laura and Ethyl, then I asked her about it.

"First of all," Sue smiled so I wouldn't be offended, "it's not a thingy. It's a nasal cannula, sometimes referred to as nasal prongs. As you can see, it's attached to this portable oxygen tank." She gestured to a small, black tank on wheels sitting close to her chair. "I have COPD. It's what brought me to Martyn Manor."

Everyone nodded their understanding but didn't pursue the topic. None of us liked to talk about why we were here. We preferred to remain in the present and show up as our best selves despite our various disabilities. This thought reminded me that I had no idea about what brought Ethyl here. She seemed the most fit in the group, both mentally and physically. I made a mental note to inquire.

Since she was on my mind, as the others talked among themselves, I noticed, really noticed, her. I'd always thought her to be unattractive. She had stringy gray hair that matched her stringy body. Since there was nothing distinctive about Ethyl's appearance, it wasn't surprising that the staff and law enforcement didn't notice her when she was in Joey's apartment the day he died.

Now that our relationship had morphed into a collegial friendship, a partnership even, I saw her through new eyes. She looked astute and engaged, eager to hear what Laura was saying. Her usual dour expression was pleasant; she even smiled from time to time, and her cheeks were pink.

I smiled to myself at the thought of rebuilding my gang. We were back to a table for four, sharing stories, and, hopefully, caring about the well-being of one another.

"Looks like the gang's all here," I said. There were smiles all around.

"I have a report," Sue said.

"Tell us," I replied.

Sue sat tall in her chair, her eyes glistened with excitement. Reporting on research was definitely her jam, as the kids would say.

"First, I looked into Agatha Esposito before moving on to the cyanide question." Sue paused to take a deep, labored breath. "When I discovered that she'd recently retired from the medical device industry, artificial knees to be exact, I looked to see if that industry had a connection to cyanide."

When Sue took another moment to catch her breath, the rest of us stared at her in anticipation.

"And, Bingo, I discovered that cyanide is connected to electroplating, which is a crucial manufacturing process used in the medical device industry for various reasons." Sue pulled a piece of paper out of her small cross-body bag. "Want to know more?"

"Sounds like that's all we need to know," Laura said.

Sue, determined to give us a full report, ignored the comment and continued. "Here's the connection. Cyanide is important in electroplating because it forms stable complexes with many metal ions, which allows for better adhesion of the plated metal, uniform plating, and control of impurities."

Setting her paper aside, Sue took another deep breath, then a bite of her BLT sandwich.

"Wow, you're some researcher!" Ethyl said.

"Thanks," Sue muttered, her mouth full of sandwich.

"So, since she worked in an industry that employed cyanide, you figure she'd know how to access it on the open market?" I asked.

Sue washed her sandwich down with a sip of iced tea. "Yes. From what I could gather, Agatha was in the procurement department and part of her job was probably buying the products needed for electroplating the knee replacement implants her company manufactured."

Ethyl pursed her lips. "Seems like the cyanide connection puts the target on Agatha. Problem is, I'm not sure what we do with this information. Do we turn it over to the detective?" She scrunched up her forehead. "Maybe he already knows."

"But if they're aware of the connection to Agatha, why are they still interrogating Martha?" Laura asked.

We'd started to attract the attention of nearby diners, so I wrapped us up. "I'll hear from Kathleen later this afternoon. She'll have a report on what she found out while doing Agatha's hair," I said. "In the meantime, let's think about what we've learned and come up with a plan when we reconvene at lunch tomorrow."

Sue did a little clapping motion with her fingers. "This is so exciting! What do we call ourselves?"

I was about to suggest the cliché of The Four Musketeers or The Four Horsewomen when Ethyl spoke up. "How about The Four Old Broads?"

Laura shook her head. "I think The Bizzy, with two z's, Broads, or maybe The Bizzy Buddies is better."

"Ahh, bizzy! How clever," replied Sue.

"Ok you two, fill us in. What does bizzy with two z's mean?" I asked.

Laura looked at Sue to respond. "If I recall correctly, the dictionary suggests that the word bizzy was first recorded in the early 20th Century and probably came from the word busy or busybody. Today it's frequently used as slang for sleuth."

"I vote for The Bizzy Buddies. People will have no idea that the spelling is different and they'll think we're just busy doing things together. Certainly not investigating a murder," I said quietly.

Looking around the room, Laura added, "It's brilliant since around here everything needs to be under wraps. We're not the only ones who are nosy."

We all left lunch with the resolve to take on the world, well, at least to be The Bizzy Buddies and continue with a possible murder investigation.

—

That afternoon, I called Kathleen. She confirmed that Agatha worked for a manufacturer of knee replacement devices, she hated Joey Russo for jilting her out of the money he owed her, and she'd temporarily moved to Martyn Manor to get him to pay up.

"Does Agatha think Joey was murdered?" I asked Kathleen.

"When I asked, she said, 'Murdered? Who said he was murdered?'"

"How did you answer?" I was concerned that Kathleen might have used my name.

Perhaps sensing my foreboding, she replied, "Don't worry, I didn't mention you. I told her I'd heard it through the grapevine. I acted all sympathetic, saying I hoped the cops weren't trying to pin a murder rap on her just because they'd caught her breaking and entering."

I thought that was pretty bold of Kathleen. "What did she say to that?"

"Apparently, she told the investigator that she'd entered Joey's apartment to retrieve some personal items she'd left behind after a recent overnight stay and that the 'powers that be' wouldn't allow her entry because it was still a crime scene."

I heard some background conversation. "I hope I'm not keeping you from your work."

"Don't worry, I'm done with appointments for the day."

"Anything else?"

"That's all I got. I don't think she told me the whole story, though. Of course, I didn't expect her to say she killed the guy, and maybe she didn't, but I think she's more involved than she's letting on."

"Thanks, Kathleen. I appreciate you doing this. I'd like to get the detective off my back, and the only way to do it is to solve the case. Murder or not, I think Agatha supplied or used cyanide in Joey's death."

We said our good-byes, and I hung up thinking that Agatha was one smart cookie. I could imagine her appealing to the police about "retrieving her personal items." Ha! She'd probably arrived for an overnight stay with just her toothbrush.

Chapter Twenty-Four

I reserved the Manor's guest apartment on Mother's Day weekend for Barbara and her family's visit, then I texted the nearby family to see if they'd like to join us for Sunday brunch. I had yet to hear back from my son Richard, or his son, Rich, but my granddaughter Susan said she and her new husband, Michael, would love to join us.

—

Monday afternoon I got a text from Harold.

> Not feeling well. Going to skip dinner. No need to bring me anything. I have supplies on hand. Perhaps you can ask one of your girlfriends to join you. Love you. 😘

> Ok. Hope you're better tomorrow. I'll check on you in the morning. Love you too.

I was concerned but not overly worried about Harold's health. He was a tough old geezer. Signing our texts with love was something new. I chuckled to myself. I did love him but marriage seemed a bit ridiculous at my age. But then, when did I worry about being ridiculous?

Harold didn't answer my text the next morning so right after breakfast, I went to his apartment and knocked. When he answered the door, I was shocked by how haggard he looked—tired, old, and seemingly off balance. "What's going on?" I asked, trying not to sound as alarmed as I felt.

With his blue chenille bathrobe flapping open, Harold stumbled over to his recliner and dropped into it. "Got chest pain, back pain, and I'm dizzy. Called my cardiologist and he's seeing me at one o'clock. My daughter's taking me."

I'd met Jennifer when she'd visited Harold from time to time. I was glad he had family nearby who cared about him. "So, you think it's your ticker?"

"Pretty sure."

I settled into Harold's comfy couch.

"Aren't you supposed to be working out?" Harold asked with his eyes half closed.

I patted the cushion next to me. "If you don't mind, I think I'll stay right here until Jennifer comes to pick you up. You don't look so good."

Harold gave me a wan smile as he slowly got up from his chair. "All right by me. I'm going to get dressed so I'm ready."

When Jennifer arrived at 12:30, I went to lunch. She promised she'd text or call me when they left the doctor's office.

By three o'clock, I was getting impatient and texted her.

> Any news?

He's getting a CT scan. Will know more in an hour or so.

At four o'clock, I called to have my dinner delivered to my apartment. I didn't want to take a chance of missing a text from Jennifer, and I wasn't confident that this time of day, I could get to the dining room and back without finding myself on a stranger's doorstep.

My dinner arrived at five o'clock. Just as I was opening the box, I had a text from Jennifer.

> They sent him to the hospital for more tests and are keeping him overnight. They think it's an aneurysm in his heart.

> Oh dear! What's the treatment?

> Open heart surgery at the worst or EVAR, a minimally invasive procedure that involves placing a stent-graft within the aorta. At his age, I'm concerned about either. There's a possibility they'll just leave it alone for now.

> Thanks for the update. Does he have his phone and a charger?

> Yes.

> Good. I'll call him tomorrow.

I prayed for Harold's recovery before tossing and turning all night.

—

If Harold being in the hospital wasn't enough, the next morning Laura arrived at breakfast with a newspaper in her hand.

"Have you seen this?" she asked.

It was Joey Russo's obituary. There wasn't much to it, except that at the end it said he died by cyanide poisoning.

"At least that fact has finally been established," I said.

"It seems like there should be an article saying the case has been solved, that's assuming it has been solved," Laura observed.

"I'll give Detective Warren a call. See what he says. By the way, Harold's in the hospital."

"Oh dear! I hope he's going to be okay. What happened?"

I filled her in with what I knew. It was times like these that I really appreciated having friends. "When I get back to my apartment, I'm going to check in on him. I'll know more at lunch."

—

When I called Harold an hour later, there was no answer. I left a voicemail asking him to call when he could.

Next, I called the precinct and asked for Detective Warren. Rather than Warren, Niles picked up the extension.

"May I help you?" she asked.

I told her who I was, that I'd read Joey Russo's obituary this morning in the newspaper, and I was wondering about the status of the case since I was a suspect. I also asked her why Warren hadn't responded to my call.

"He's on administrative leave. The case is still open and, as far as I know, you're still a suspect."

Surprised by this revelation about Warren, I asked why.

Niles quietly answered. "I'm afraid I can't comment on that. Anything else?"

"Has murder been ruled out?" I asked.

Niles gave me more than I thought she would. "Although the autopsy determined the cause of death to be cyanide poisoning, we have yet to find evidence of foul play. The only fingerprints on the glass of liquid containing the poison belonged to Mr. Russo."

"So, are you considering it a suicide?" I asked.

"We're still investigating."

"What's going to happen to Agatha Esposito?" I wondered if they knew about her cyanide connection.

"That will be for the judge to decide. She may come to an agreement with Martyn Manor in which case, the charges of breaking and entering will be dropped."

I started to ask a follow-up question but Niles interrupted me.

"I've said more than I should because I believe you were unjustly targeted, but I have nothing else to say about the case. Have a good day, Mrs. Anderson."

With that, my phone went dead.

I jumped when my phone immediately rang. "Hello?"

It was Elizabeth saying she was coming for Mother's Day and Ruth would be joining her.

"My goodness! A regular family reunion. That's lovely."

"We'll stay at the Marriott Courtyard. Ruth has points there. I understand the girls are staying at the Manor."

"Yes," I confirmed. "Have you heard from Richard or Rich? Susan and Michael said they're coming."

"Not yet, but don't worry, they'll be there." Elizabeth was the only one in the family who could push Richard around if the need arose.

Elizabeth continued. "Shadows on the Hudson has a Sunday Brunch. I checked out their website. I'll make reservations if that's all right with you."

"Of course. I'd also like to invite Harold and his family. I'll text you a final count after I issue the invitation. Right now, Harold is in the hospital but I'm hoping for a full recovery." I explained his condition to my daughter.

"I'm sorry to hear that. Keep me posted," she said. "Sounds like this relationship has gone up a notch."

"As a matter of fact, he's asked me to marry him."

I heard my daughter take in her breath. "My goodness! Did you say yes?"

"Not yet. I'm deliberating. Do you have an opinion on the subject?"

I could imagine Elizabeth zipping her lips. "Not me. I just want you to be happy."

"Good response," I snickered into the phone. "See you in May. Thanks for calling. Love you."

I couldn't believe that I'd suggested inviting Harold's whole family. Was I subconsciously turning this brunch into a wedding reception? Had I made a decision after all? Was marriage still on the table with Harold's new diagnosis?

Before I could put my phone down, a group text came through to everyone in my family. It was from Elizabeth.

Family Reunion and Mother's Day Brunch to honor our mom, grandmother, and great-grandmother. Sunday, May 11, noon at Shadows On The Hudson. Reservations will be made in three days. RSVP to this text ASAP.

Elizabeth didn't let moss grow under her feet, as my dad would say. She was a woman of action who took no prisoners.

—

Later that morning, I decided to take a walk around the grounds instead of going to the workout room. It was a beautiful, early spring day, and I needed to clear my head. I'd pushed the information about Warren to the back burner so I could concentrate on my personal life for now. I intended to use this quiet time to think.

The pair of swans had returned and were swimming around the lake, birds were singing, and the air smelled of blooming trees. Before I left my apartment, Alexa told me the temperature was sixty-nine degrees with sun. I was comfortable in my old trench coat, and the sun felt good on my shoulders.

When my phone pinged, I sat down on a bench next to the water to check my messages. There was a text from Harold's granddaughter, Sarah.

> Grandpa asked me to text you. I'm picking him up from the hospital and taking him back to his apartment. He'll fill you in on the details. We should be there right after lunch.

> Thanks for letting me know. Give him my love.

The text seemed like good news. At least they weren't preparing him for surgery. I closed my eyes, bowed my head, and thanked God for sparing Harold. Of course, this didn't mean he was all right, but it was encouraging. As I sat in the sunshine, I whispered another prayer. "So, what do you think, God? Should I marry the old guy?"

When I looked up, I saw a red cardinal perched on a nearby tree. He chirped loudly and his mate flew in to join him. Since cardinals frequently mate for life, seeing them together seemed like another sign.

Chapter Twenty-Five

I went back to my apartment after lunch and impatiently waited for Harold to text me. There was no point in mulling over the decision about whether or not to get married if the offer was now off the table. Unexpected circumstances with one's health changed things.

> I'm back. Come on down. Door's unlocked.

Harold had only been out of my sight for a little over twenty-four hours, but it felt like days. When I arrived at his apartment, he was dressed in a navy blue jumpsuit, relaxing in his recliner. He lowered his legs and I leaned in to give him a kiss.

"Welcome back. Glad you're home," I said.

"Yeah, at least I'm not as 'dead as a door nail' as your dad would say." Harold chuckled to himself. "They gave me a reprieve from any drastic measures to see what's going to happen next."

"What are the possibilities?"

"If this damn aneurysm stays like it is," he patted his chest, "then I'm good to go on with my life as usual. Well, except for no lifting, or jogging, or extra strenuous activities, but otherwise.…"

"And if it doesn't?"

"If in six months they do another scan and it's grown, then they'll have to do something about it. I'm going to cross that bridge when I come to it." He gave me a half-hearted smile. "One day at a time, right?"

"Right. How are you feeling?"

"I'm better. They put me on meds so my symptoms are gone. Not quite fit as a fiddle, but I will be soon. I'm counting on it."

"Always the optimist," I said.

"Yep. What's new with you?"

"Detective Warren is on administrative leave. Niles was all hush-hush about it."

"That's interesting. What are your thoughts on that?"

"I haven't had time to process it yet. I've been busy thinking about other things," I replied.

"Anything I should know about?" Harold asked.

I squirmed on the couch cushion. Apparently, squirming was my tic when I had something important to ask. Harold's tic was clearing his throat. "Is your marriage proposal still on the table?"

"Of course it is!" Harold turned in his chair so he could look me squarely in the eyes. "Have you made a decision?"

"Yes."

"Yes you've made a decision, or the decision is yes? I'm old, you gotta be crystal clear or I won't get it." Harold winked at me. He was a charming old guy.

"The answer is yes, I'll marry you."

Harold got up from his chair and came over to sit next to me. I think he wanted to be sure he was hearing correctly.

"Really?"

"Yes, really. Now kiss me and seal the deal."

Harold pulled me into his arms and kissed me. When I clung to him, I realized just how scared I was, thinking I could lose him.

When I pulled back, I asked, "What about May eleventh? Is a little over a month too short a notice?" When Harold seemed speechless, I continued. "My whole family is coming to town to celebrate Mother's Day. We're having brunch at Shadows on the Hudson…"

Harold interrupted. "That's a really cool place with a great view."

"May I continue?" I gave him a little punch. I was the one who usually interrupted him.

"Sorry."

"Wedding or not, I'd like to invite your family. But, since everyone will be there, I thought we could have a short ceremony on the veranda, then go inside for a wedding brunch. What do you say?"

"I'm speechless. When did you come up with all this? Not twenty-four hours ago you were undecided."

I gave him a peck on the cheek. "I decided about an hour ago. The rest just fell into place. I talked with Elizabeth yesterday. Barbara, Bobbie, and Marti were already planning on coming for Mother's Day, then it snowballed into my whole family. When I asked Elizabeth to add you and your family to the reservations, I realized that I'd made a decision—whether I knew it or not." I put my head on Harold's shoulder. "Plus, I saw a pair of cardinals today."

"You what?"

"Never mind." I gave my head a little shake. I needed to stay on point. "So, what do you think?"

"I think it's a wonderful plan. Time's a wasting, no sense in waiting. May eleventh, huh?" Harold looked like a deer in headlights. I'd shocked him before but this was a doozy.

"Marcella can be our flower girl. We'll need witnesses, but we can bypass having attendants. It will be casual. You can wear your going-out-to-dinner clothes. I'll wear the dress I wore for Captain's Night on the cruise. Let's have spring flowers on the tables. What are your favorites?"

"We're already talking about flowers? I thought weddings took months to plan."

"Not this one. Once we decide on flowers and you text your kids and I text mine, I think we're done." I took Harold's hand. "Need time to think about all this? I know how you like to mull things over."

Harold shook his head. "Not this time. I'm on board with it all." When he paused, I wondered what he was thinking.

"How about daisies and pink roses? And I'm going to wear my funeral suit if you're going to be all fancy."

"Perfect."

Harold squeezed my hand. "Now let's text our families and get this ball rolling before you change your mind."

I narrowed my eyes and looked over at him. "Am I a woman who changes her mind about important issues, Mr. Lancaster?"

"Not so far as I know, Mrs. Soon-to-be-Lancaster."

Before we group texted our children and adult grands, I called the venue to reserve the veranda and a room for the reception. Apparently, Mother's Day wasn't popular for weddings so both were available. After I hung up, I gave Harold the thumbs up and we sent out our texts.

> You're invited to the wedding of Martha Anderson and Harold Lancaster on May 11 at Shadows on the Hudson, Poughkeepsie, New York.

> The wedding will be on the veranda at 10:30 followed by brunch at 11:00.

> Please RSVP as soon as possible.

When both of our phones rang immediately, we muted them. It was a mutual decision to let our impromptu, if not shocking, invitation sink in before we addressed any questions or concerns.

"You look like you need a nap. I'll ask the dining room to deliver both of our dinners here tonight. See you at five." With that, I gave Harold a kiss and left his apartment. We both needed time to digest our plans.

—

I'd just made a life-altering decision and what did I do when I got back to my apartment? I went straight to my closet and pulled out the purple lace dress I'd worn on the transcontinental cruise I'd taken with my granddaughter. No one I knew except Susan had seen it, and I didn't want to go to the trouble of shopping for something new. I tried it on and looked at myself in the mirror. The jacket was a nice touch for a daytime wedding, the color was perfect, and it still fit.

—

Before I broke the news to my friends about marrying Harold and my plans to move to a studio that would adjoin his apartment, I told the crew about Detective Warren being on administrative leave.

"What does that mean for the case?" Laura asked.

"I don't know. Niles said I was still on the suspect's list, she confirmed that cyanide was used, and only Russo's prints were on the glass. But" I looked at my friends, "the case is still open."

I rushed ahead before anyone had time to go down the speculation road. "Also, Harold and I are getting married in a few weeks and I'm moving to a studio which will adjoin his apartment."

When I sat back to take a breath, I noticed a woman at a nearby table giving us the side-eye. Was she listening in? What business was my marriage of hers anyway? I'd seen her around, of course, but I didn't know her name. I put her to the back of my mind when Sue began to speak.

Sue was the least stunned by my announcement and responded with, "If you need someone to marry you, I've officiated at weddings in the past. In New York, I'll need a one-day license and to register with the city. You'll need to get your marriage license first." Sue held up her hand. "Just a suggestion. You probably have this all figured out already."

When we all looked at her, she turned pink and sipped her iced tea.

"This was a very impromptu decision. We only have the venue. Obviously, we haven't thought about some of the details. Let me ask Harold. Thanks for the offer."

Ethyl shook her head from side to side. "I had no idea this was in the works. I hope you know what you're doing." Perhaps remembering her new kinder persona, she added, "I'm really happy for you and Harold. How is he, by the way?"

"He's better. On hold for six months, then they'll know more."

I looked at my three new buddies. "By the way, you're all invited to the wedding and the brunch following."

Ethyl had the biggest smile.

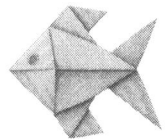

Chapter Twenty-Six

That afternoon, before I went to Harold's for dinner, I rummaged around in my end table drawer for a small notebook. I needed to keep track of wedding details.

Maybe I was too old for this. I could barely remember friends' names or how to get to my apartment. Was I capable of organizing a wedding, a reception brunch, and a move? All while tracking an in-house mystery?

When I found the notebook I wrote down: Get wedding license, order flowers, ask Harold about using Sue as officiate, return calls from family, make hair and nail appointments, sign prenuptial agreements.

Next, I called Jeff in admissions to make arrangements for me to move to the studio and for them to open a door into Harold's apartment. He assured me that my studio and the door would be ready for an early-May move-in.

I figured I'd make the most difficult call first. My son's texts had been the most urgent.

"Good afternoon, Richard. I'm returning your texts."

"Mother, why didn't you speak with me about getting married?"

"I decided rather on the spur of the moment. Once the decision was made, we sent out the invitation since the event is coming up so fast."

"The event! The wedding you mean."

"Yes, the wedding followed by a brunch. Barbara and her family were already scheduled to come for Mother's Day, and then Elizabeth and Ruth decided to tag along, so everyone was already coming. It seemed like an ideal time."

"The timing isn't the point. Do you really think marriage is the right decision for a woman your age? What about a prenup? Have you considered this?"

"As a matter of fact, I have. Would you be willing to draw one up for us? It's very straightforward. All my assets go to my family upon my death, all of Harold's go to his. If he precedes me in death, I will receive widow benefits from the government. See? Simple. Could you draw it up before you come for lunch next time?"

"Of course, but what about living arrangements? I don't think Martyn Manor is a safe place for either of you. In fact, I've spoken with the admissions director at The Landing and they have an opening. I think both of you should move there."

"I had planned on speaking to you in person about that, but since you brought it up…." I explained our plans and told him about my taking over the monthly bill for a studio.

"But Ruth, Elizabeth, and I have that all arranged. Can you actually afford the monthly payments?"

"Since you so generously paid my entry fee, I can afford the payments on the studio. I'll pick up the bill starting in June. If the three of you would like to make one last gesture, you can share the cost of our wedding reception. It can be your gift to us. The wedding is the bride's responsibility after all. If everyone can come, there will be about twenty-five in attendance."

"I'll discuss all this with the girls. I still think you should move, but I guess I have no choice but to leave that up to you and Harold." Richard paused. "I'll come to lunch on the fifteenth."

"That's fine. I'll put you down for April 15, tax day. See you then. Bye."

"Goodbye, Mother."

Relieved that call had been made, I called the rest of the family. Those conversations were short and sweet. They were all excited about the wedding and looking forward to meeting Harold's family. If they had trepidations, they kept them to themselves.

I had one last call to make. Although I rarely spoke with Molly these days, she represented the friends I'd lost, and I wanted to invite her to our wedding. She sounded a little jealous. I think she'd hoped to be married long before now, but she graciously responded. "I'll be there with bells on. Thanks for the invitation, Martha. Congratulations to you and Harold."

—

Four hours later, when I left my apartment to go to Harold's for dinner, there was a package leaning against the wall next to my door. I thought it was odd because packages were generally left in the mailroom. I didn't want to keep Harold waiting, so I set the package inside the door and made my way to his apartment while I still had my faculties.

I paused in front of the door to the studio I would be moving into soon. Was I ready for a move?

"Have you talked with your family yet?" Harold asked as soon as we settled around the table and opened our take-out boxes.

"I have."

"And…"

"My son was predictably outraged that a woman my age would consider getting married. Our conversation led to my moving and the new financial arrangement. I'd hoped to do that in person. I told him if he wanted to make one last gesture, he and the girls could pick up the bill for our reception."

Harold looked aghast. "You didn't!"

"Why not? The wedding is the responsibility of the bride and her family. It's only about twenty-five people, so it's not going to be a fortune. They can always say no."

The count for the brunch reminded me to ask Harold a question. "Besides your family, is there anyone else you'd like to invite?"

Harold gave me the names of three buddies he hung out with. I pulled my notebook from my purse and added them to the list. He'd seemed to have lost interest in challenging me about the brunch bill.

"By the way, how did your family take the news?" I asked.

"They were all delighted," Harold replied. "And why wouldn't they be?"

Worried that I might not find my way home, Harold walked me back to my apartment after dinner. He'd mostly regained his strength and was almost back to normal.

When I walked through the door, I was surprised to see the box I'd thrown in earlier. I locked and bolted the door, set my purse on the table, and pulled out my scissors. The box was about the size of a toaster but it was mostly filled with crunched-up newspaper. In the middle of the paper was an orange origami fish made of intricately folded paper. It was the size of a small saucer. I carefully examined the object but couldn't find a message. As much as I hated to destroy the design, I finally unfolded the fish. When I laid the paper flat, I saw words written in a tight script.

If you're planning on using Russo's stash to pay for your wedding, shame on you! If you know what's good for you, put the money or jewels or whatever in this box and leave it in front of Russo's door. Do it NOW! You wouldn't want my brothers to pay you a visit!!

Another threat, and this time, I knew it wasn't from Russo. The wording about the brothers sounded familiar. Where had I heard it before? Was this threat serious enough to involve the police? Although I knew Harold probably wasn't asleep yet, I decided to wait and tell him later. No sense worrying him this late at night.

I crawled into bed, still racking my brain about the note. In a few minutes I still felt uneasy, so I got out of bed and padded back into the living room to make sure the door was locked and the bolt was firmly in place. I even checked the windows.

When I got back into bed, I asked Alexa to play relaxing music for eight minutes. Before I drifted off to sleep, I wondered what kind of person would go to the trouble to send a note like that. A little voice in my head said, "A person determined to get their hands on Joey's stash—that's who!"

Chapter Twenty-Seven

Unlike the time I thought I heard someone enter my apartment during the night and later questioned my memory, this time I had physical evidence.

I examined the note again before I left for lunch. The handwriting was dense and precise. An accountant, perhaps? The use of an origami figure and the threat of attacking brothers still had me baffled. I put the note in my purse along with my phone and door key.

After Laura, Ethyl, Sue, and I had settled down with our lunches, I pulled out the orange paper and read the message out loud. Laura immediately noticed the folds. "Was this an origami figure?" she asked.

She was one astute lady. "Yes. It was a fish. Know anyone who makes origami objects?"

Ignoring my question, Ethyl asked one of her own. "What about the threat? The bit about the brothers sounds ominous. Maybe you should contact the police."

"I've been racking my brain about that. Sounds familiar, but I can't place where I've heard it before. It seems strange that this person knows about our wedding. Besides our families, you're the only people we've told."

Sue looked at the nearby tables. "Lots of big ears in this place."

Ethyl pointed. "Speaking of, who's that?"

We all looked. "I've seen her before but she might be new," I said. "Maybe Sophia will assign her to me."

When everyone dismissed the unknown lady, I added, "I'll show the note to Harold tonight, then call Detective Niles tomorrow. Maybe by then something will jog my memory."

Laura left the table saying she needed a nap, and Sue followed her out. I lingered with Ethyl. "Want some ice cream?" I asked.

"Sure, you buying?" she quipped.

"Cone or cup?"

"Cone. Chocolate."

I left to get two ice cream cones. When I returned, I held mine aloft. "To Spring."

"To Spring," Ethyl replied, looking toward the sunny windows.

Beyond toasting Spring, I wanted to know Ethyl's story, but I wasn't sure how to approach her. She always clammed up when anyone asked about her past. I opened with, "You were here when I moved in. How long have you lived at the Manor?"

"I'm a rare original. It's going on six years already. Do you think that's some kind of record?" Ethyl looked at me with a sheepish grin.

"Maybe. Out of my original five friends, three have died, one returned home to Canada, and one has been taken over by the opposite sex."

"Is that what's going to happen after you and Harold get married?" Ethyl asked, her voice low, her expression sad.

"Of course not! My life will roll along much as it is now. I'd never abandon my girlfriends for a man like Molly did." Ethyl was good at putting the ball back in my court but I pushed on. "Where did you live before coming here?"

"I lived in Baton Rouge, Louisiana. When I was diagnosed with OABD, my stepson moved me here. At the time, he lived in Poughkeepsie but he has since moved to Minneapolis."

I took a lick of my ice cream cone. I didn't want to bombard Ethyl with questions, but it was hard not to. "What's OABD?"

"It's a bipolar disorder in older adults. Older-Age Bipolar Disorder or OABD. Get it?"

"I get the letters but what are the symptoms? You seem fairly normal to me." I gave her a side-eye glance. "At least now that we're friends."

Ethyl ignored the little barb. "Basically, it means that I'm easily depressed. Unlike younger people with a bipolar condition, I have few manic symptoms but more depressive episodes. I used to isolate in my apartment for days at a time. My depression caused me to show up as an angry, mean person. They bring me my medication every morning to make sure I take it, but I can still be suddenly bombarded with a deep depression that's difficult to come out of."

She looked thoughtful for a minute then added, "Having lunch with you three has helped me maintain a sense of normalcy and forced me to move past my dark feelings. At least most of the time."

Ethyl suddenly stopped talking and her face grew red. I reached out and patted her hand. "Sharing all that took a lot of courage. Thanks."

After taking a breath, Ethyl added, "I guess my stepson didn't want a suicide on his conscience, so he moved me in here. I felt dumped and I was angry. It's taken me a long time, but I'm finally recognizing that moving to the Manor was the best course of action." Ethyl's lips turned up a tiny bit. "Besides, who else would have gotten you in trouble with Agnes?"

"Harold and I should thank you for being a snitch. We met in Duly's office that day. Did you know that?"

"No." Ethyl took a lick at her cone. "You're welcome."

"Any family? Did you have a career? Do you like cats, dogs, or neither?" I tried to lighten up what might have felt like an interrogation.

"I like dogs. Big, floppy-eared dogs with wagging tails and smiley faces."

"That's specific."

"Well, I had a dog like that when I was a kid." Ethyl came back to my questions. "No family to speak of. I was adopted as a baby and I have no idea who my birth parents were. I was an only child. My parents died in a car accident when I was twenty-two. I've been on my own ever since, except for a brief marriage to Edgar, who died twenty years ago. We never had children, but it was Edgar's son from a previous marriage who moved me here. Edgar had Alzheimer's and I took care of him until his death. His son Rudy greatly appreciated me caring for his father, so he's kept me under his wing in recent years."

Ethyl paused as if thinking. "To answer your final, I hope…." She gave me a look, "question, I'm a retired schoolteacher. Junior high algebra mostly. Squashing her ice cream into her cone with her tongue, Ethyl concluded. "See? Nothing very interesting."

"Of course, your past life is interesting," I said with emotion. "It's made you who you are, and now I have a better understanding of what makes you tick. Thanks for sharing."

We finished our ice cream cones and left the cafeteria. "What about you?" Ethyl asked as we walked to our apartments.

"My life's theme is threes. I had three sisters, I have three children, Elizabeth, Ruth, and Richard, and three grandchildren, Rich, Susan, and Barbara. I've had three husbands, Kevin, Marvin, and Peter. I hail from Iowa, and I was a social worker and a stay-at-home mom. I like to embroider, read and listen to books, solve mysteries, watch football, and get into good trouble," I said, summing up ninety years of living.

To give my life a little color, I added, "I like dogs, fall flowers, and all things French." I looked at Ethyl. "And I highly value interesting women who happen to show up in my life." I gave her a little poke. "Even when they first show up as scalawags, as my dad would say."

"Me too," Ethyl choked out. Her eyes were glistening. "The interesting women bit." Turning to her door and pulling out her key, she added, "See you tomorrow," she paused, "if the creek don't rise."

Chapter Twenty-Eight

When I showed Harold the threatening note, he didn't respond like I thought he would.

"Maybe you should leave the box by Russo's door with your mini cam set up on the opposite wall." I wondered why I hadn't thought of that. "Or, maybe you should just call the detective and wash your hands of the whole thing."

He didn't seem open to discussion as he immediately launched into plans about getting our marriage license and other wedding details. This was a man on a mission to get married. To hell with a murder mystery unfolding under his nose.

—

We decided to take Sue up on her offer to officiate. I would have preferred a pastor, but since we didn't personally know any in Poughkeepsie, Sue would have to do. She was delighted when I gave her the news and promised to be ready on the day of the ceremony.

—

Apparently I too was swept away with wedding plans, because the next morning I put the call to Niles on the back burner as I busied myself looking at photos of Marti in the sailor suit her mothers said she was going to wear to the wedding and a video of Marcella in a pink frilly dress prancing around as she practiced being our flower girl and ring bearer.

We'd decided against any of our children serving as attendants. The family dynamics around the choice felt like a minefield. Since Marcella was already standing up front, she could have our rings tucked into a drawstring bag located at the bottom of her flower basket. It made sense and sounded easy. Marcella was now nine years old and quite mature for her age. It wasn't like having a preschooler who might decide to sit midway down the aisle.

I pursed online photos of bouquets traditionally carried by the bride but decided on carrying five white roses with stems wrapped in satin, one each for my sisters and parents, so I could feel their presence.

Harold had sent notes to his guy friends inviting them to the wedding. When they confirmed the invitation, I promptly forwarded the new count to the venue.

—

Richard arrived early for our lunch on the fifteenth so he could go over the prenuptial agreement he'd prepared for Harold and me. It was straightforward, and we signed our documents on the spot. After the three of us had lunch, Richard took us to our scheduled appointment at the City Clerk's office to obtain our marriage license. We had our birth certificates and current photo IDs in hand. I brought a copy of my divorce decree from my first husband and the death certificates for my second and third.

When we got back to the car, I assured Harold that the flowers had been ordered along with napkins with our names and wedding date engraved on them. "I know it's cheesy, but I couldn't resist," I told him.

"Would you mind dropping us off at Zimmer Brothers Jewelers? We'll Uber back," Harold asked Richard as he pulled away from the curb.

"Of course," my son replied.

"We need to pick out rings," Harold explained.

Riding through town with the sun shining through the back window, I suddenly remembered the dream I'd had the night before. Missy had appeared in a flowing white gown, her hair shimmering in the cloud-filled sky. She was more of an essence than a presence. I reached out and tried to touch her, but it was like touching a shadow. She hummed a little tune I didn't recognize then said, "Be happy, Marte," before evaporating into the clouds. Marte was a nickname from long ago. Missy adopted it when she heard my story of living in the Paris neighborhood of Montmartre.

The memory of my dream caused me to fiddle with the ring she gifted me just before she died. Harold noticed. He doesn't miss much.

"Thinking about Missy?" he asked.

"I dreamed about her last night and it just came back to me."

"Want to share?"

I told him about the dream. "I think she means us. She loved me beyond the usual friend-to-friend kind of love."

I looked at Harold to see his reaction. His eyebrows went up a notch.

"And?" he prompted.

"And, although I felt an unusual attraction to her, I wasn't interested in having a," I lowered my voice even further, "lesbian relationship."

Thank goodness Richard was having a robust hands-free phone conversation in the front seat.

"I guess thinking about rings reminded me of this one," I raised my little finger, "and my special bond with Missy. I don't need her blessing but the confirmation that she wants me happy, which I believe partially means marrying you, gives me a warm feeling." I looked at Harold. "Does that make sense?"

He took my hand. "Absolutely."

"Since we're on the subject," I took a breath and whispered in Harold's ear. "When you were abducted by your son, Detective Warren accused me of having a three-way with you and Missy. That's why he thought I'd abducted you."

"W-h-a-t?"

I put my finger to my lips. "Shhh."

"I'll fill you in with the details later." I pointed to the front seat. "Richard just ended his call."

"Sorry about taking that phone call, Mother. I know you like drivers to give their full attention to the road." He looked at me through the rearview mirror. "That was Rich saying he and his family will be at the wedding. I rarely hear from him." Richard said by way of explanation.

We picked out our rings. A lovely white gold wedding band with a diamond in the middle for me, a plain gold band for Harold.

Just three weeks to the wedding and I was feeling nervous. Had I made the right decision? Would marrying Harold complicate my life more than enhance it? What would living together be like? Maybe Richard was right. Maybe I was too old for this kind of tomfoolery, as my dad would say.

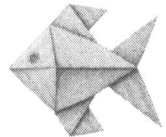

Chapter Twenty-Nine

I made an appointment to have my hair cut and colored. I didn't want it to look "newly done" for the big day, so I decided to go two weeks before the wedding. The day was chilly for April and I wore my trench coat. Jake picked me up at the curb.

"What's up, Mrs. A?" he asked.

"I'm getting married," I replied nonchalantly.

Without missing a beat, Jake said, "Congratulations! When's the big day?"

"May seventh."

I appreciated not having further conversation on the topic. It seemed that most people had an opinion, and I was growing weary listening to their responses.

I gingerly left the minivan, drawing my coat up around my neck. The sky had darkened and rain was threatening. With the wind at my back, I sailed through the door of the salon. Kathleen greeted me with her usual warm smile. "Good to see you, Martha. Have a seat."

When I sat down in Kathleen's chair, my eyes immediately went to an origami figure nestled next to her purple crystal on the counter. "What's that?" I asked, pointing to the yellow object.

"It's an origami crab," she replied. "Clever, don't you think?"

"Clever," I replied. "Did you make it?"

"Oh no. Agatha, that red-haired lady you sent my way, made it for me."

"Agatha Esposito gave that to you?" I asked, my voice raised.

"Yes. Isn't that just what I said?" Kathleen gave me a strange look. "What's the matter?"

"I recently received an origami from an unknown source. When I opened it all the way, there was a message written on the paper."

"What did it say?"

I paused, trying to remember the exact words. "It said something about Harold and me using Russo's—you know, the guy that died— stash to pay for our wedding and if I didn't put the money in a box and leave it in front of what once was Russo's door, this person would send her brothers after me…something like that. Very threatening."

When Kathleen didn't respond right away, I added, "I've been racking my brain about the brother thing and now I remember. Agatha used the same threat on Rosa Russo, Joey Russo's wife at the time, when Rosa confronted her about having an affair with her husband."

Holding the brush she used for applying color in mid-air, Kathleen exclaimed, "Good grief! Does this mean Agatha murdered Joey? Is she sending her brothers to hurt you? Did you show the note to the police? Do you know anything about this stash?"

I paused before answering, giving Kathleen time to collect herself; she was usually so calm. "The note doesn't necessarily mean Agatha killed Joey, it just means she really, and I mean no matter what it takes, really wants whatever she thinks he hid away. I doubt if she'll send her brothers to hurt me. They're in Brooklyn for heaven's sake." I thought for a moment. "And they're probably old."

"What about the police? Are they doing anything about this?" Kathleen prompted. She'd calmed down and had resumed putting goop on my hair.

"I haven't notified them yet," I said sheepishly. "I've been preoccupied with wedding plans. They rarely take me seriously anyway."

"And the stash?"

I put my hand on my black plastic-caped heart. "I absolutely have no knowledge of a stash. Harold saw Joey making a capsule of some sort, but that's all I know. There may not even be a stash."

Since Kathleen's next client had yet to appear, I stayed in her chair. We weren't done talking. "What did Agatha say when she gave you the origami?"

Kathleen picked up the folded crab and studied it before returning it to the counter. "She said she made me the crab because of my July birthday. I happened to mention it when she was here."

"Any news about her breaking and entering case?" I asked.

"She said her lawyer negotiated with the Manor's lawyer and settled the case against her out of court. I guess they were convinced that she entered the apartment to pick up her things. Even though it was an illegal entry, they let her off with a slap on the wrist and a warning to stay away from Martyn Manor."

"Figures."

"Maybe if you showed the police the note you received and told them about my crab, they'd re-arrest her."

I closed my eyes for a moment. The fumes from the coloring solution weren't helping my dry eye condition. "Or maybe they'd think I was a doddering old fool. Don't forget, they accused me once of abducting Harold and," I paused for emphasis, "I'm on their list of suspects for Russo's possible murder. I'm thinking that keeping a low profile might be my best bet. What I'm wondering is…" I paused to remember the unknown lady in the cafeteria.

"Yes?"

"What I'm wondering is who's Agatha's inside person? Someone overheard me telling my friends about our wedding and passed it on. Maybe it's the same person who told Russo that I had dinner with his ex-wife."

While I was busy considering this, Kathleen picked up her crab and started unfolding it. "Look!" She held up the flat paper.

There was writing on the unfolded paper. *A friend of Martha's is no friend of mine. Beware!*

"Another threat," Kathleen said. She was cooler this time. Perhaps spending years with a wayward husband had given her some perspective if the threat was directed toward her.

Kathleen ushered me out of her chair. Her next client had appeared. "Sounds like we have a mutual enemy and you have a mole in your facility, Martha. Do you know how to get rid of moles?"

"No, do you?"

"You put bait in a trap. That's how."

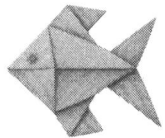

Chapter Thirty

"Bob offered us his place in the Poconos for our honeymoon. What do you think?" Harold asked me at dinner. It was Taco Tuesday, and I was trying to figure out how to bite into my overstuffed fish taco.

"Is Scotty going to beam us up there?" I countered.

Harold gave me a look. Head lowered, eyes lifted, mouth puckered. "My daughter said she'd drive us and my granddaughter can pick us up if we return on Saturday or Sunday."

"That's very kind of them. Remind me where in the Poconos his place is?" All I could think of was Audrey in Bob's bed while her husband tried to call her. She was a renter here who took advantage of our friend Bob and his kindness. The Poconos didn't elicit positive feelings for me.

"His cottage is on Lake Wallenpaupack, near the town of Hawley. There are twenty-three hospitals within fifty miles of the place, just in case you're wondering." Harold sat back and took a sip of his sangria. A look of satisfaction on his rather handsome-for-an-old-guy face.

"I can see you've done your homework. I guess this means you want to go. You're not worried about your heart?"

Harold thumped his chest. "It's either going to work or it isn't. Doesn't much matter where I am. Dying while lying next to you in a cottage on a lake in the Poconos wouldn't be the worst thing in the world."

"Who said I'd be lying next to you?" I gave him a sweet smile so he'd know I was teasing. "Are there lots of stairs? How long is the car ride? What's the duration of our stay? How do we get groceries? Who's doing the cooking? Don't forget, I burnt the pot the last time I was allowed in a real kitchen." My mind was whirling both with the excitement of getting away and the risks we'd be taking. "You know, the Devil is in the details."

"Is that a Dadism?"

"No, it's a Marthaism. Stop avoiding my questions."

Harold wiped his mouth with his napkin. Tacos were so messy. "The trip takes less than two hours. Bob says there are steep stairs down to the dock, but otherwise, it's mostly on one level with extra bedrooms upstairs. I'll take one of the upstairs bedrooms if you'd like to have your own room on the main floor." Harold fiddled around with his beans and rice.

"Go on."

"I thought we'd stay a week. Go the day after the wedding and return the following Sunday. That's unless your family is staying after the wedding. In that case, we could go the following week."

Harold was about to explain the food situation when I noticed the Strange Lady watching us from a table just behind Harold. She was the same one who had been eavesdropping on my friends and me at lunch.

I held up my finger. "Hold on a second." I lowered my voice to a whisper. "Don't look now, but do you know the woman in the gray dress at the table behind you? She's very intent on listening to our conversation. She acted the same way at lunch. I think she's The Mole."

Harold shifted in his seat but resisted the urge to turn around. "The what?"

"The Mole." I explained to Harold what Kathleen and I had discussed and what she'd said about the best way to catch a mole. "With bait in a trap," I summed up.

"Are you trying to avoid our discussion about the Poconos? You know, if you don't want to go, you can just say so," Harold huffed.

"No, I'm not avoiding anything. I'm just noticing the woman. Drop your napkin so you'll have a reason to look around."

"Good grief, Martha. Must you always be in investigator mode?" Harold asked just before he dutifully dropped his napkin, gave the woman behind him a good once over, then returned to his sangria. "Don't know her. Do you?"

"No, but I'm going to find out who she is…" I looked at Harold, who definitely wasn't smiling. "…after we get back from the Poconos."

"So, we're going?" Harold's smile showed off his new crown.

"Sure, why not? I'll leave the food situation up to you. I can exist a long time on Honey Crisp apples and peanut butter. But" I pointed at Harold, "it has to be Skippy Extra Crunchy."

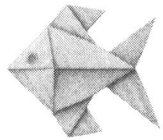

Chapter Thirty-One

A week before the wedding I felt nervous but ready. I wondered if all brides were nervous, no matter their age. Before my marriage to Kevin at the tender age of twenty-one, I was worried about sex. Would I get pregnant despite being fitted for a diaphragm? Would intercourse be as mind-blowing (in a good way) as I had imagined it? Would I make my husband happy?

Different questions emerged with marriage number two. Would my marriage to Marvin also end in divorce? Had I learned enough lessons from my first experience to make this one successful? I knew it wasn't only up to me, but I wanted to bring all I could to the table. Was I too old to get married again? I was only fifty-five but at the time, that seemed old to be getting married. I was also concerned about my grown children. Would they accept this new person into our family?

When Marvin died suddenly after just over a year into our marriage, one of my biggest concerns about marrying again was whether or not Peter would make me a widow. Marryin' and buryin' wasn't a picnic, so I didn't want to repeat the scenario. Fortunately, Peter lived a good long time but he still died before I did so here I was, once again a widow who was about to get married. Who in their right mind gets married four times anyway?

Just for the heck of it, I Googled the question. Of course, numerous celebrities like Jennifer Lopez, Ben Affleck, and Kelsey Grammar had been married multiple times. Zsa Zsa Gabor had been married nine times, for heaven's sake! Most, if not all, of these marriages ended in divorce. I also discovered that in 2024, Marjorie Fiterman, age 102, married Bernie Pittman, 100. They dated for nine years, so I guess they knew what they were doing.

Harold and I had known each other for a little over three years but during that time, I said I'd never marry again and we weren't in a committed relationship. The memory of Missy and me smoking weed on my bed came to mind, followed by the divine evening when I drank wine with a sexy Frenchman who was also a ship's captain. Unfortunately, I couldn't remember his name.

Even though my memory for names of people and places was dwindling, say nothing of how to get from one place to another, at least my memory of events seemed to still be intact. I could hear the Captain's French accent as if we'd spoken yesterday, and I could still smell Missy's alluring perfume.

My mind circled back to Marjorie and Bernie. I wondered if they were still alive and married? There were photos of them on the Internet. They looked pretty feeble on their wedding day. Harold and I looked young in comparison.

To clear my mind, I took out my journal, the little book where I kept track of wedding details. I went to a clean page. I needed to write down all the things that were circling around in my mind about the Russo Case. Harold was right. I needed to leave my investigator-self behind.

1. Forget about the origami notes to me and Kathleen

2. Forget about the strange, nosy lady who is possibly a mole

3. Forget about Agatha's threat of sending her brothers to hurt me

4. Stop wondering whether or not Joey was murdered

5. Stop considering the best place to position a minicam outside of Joey's apartment

Next, I made a list of the things I needed to be thinking about instead.

1. Start packing for our honeymoon (weird to use that term)

2. Start packing for the move to my new apartment

3. Decide what to give Harold for a wedding gift

This last item on the list came up because Harold said he was getting us matching leather recliners as wedding gifts. "The fancy kind with buttons for the footrest and headrest. Even a place to plug in your phone," he'd said. I was putting my current recliner in my studio apartment and Harold was donating his to the Salvation Army.

Since Barbara and Bobbie were coming before the wedding and staying at the Manor, I decided to ask them to help me pack for the trip to the Poconos and the move. I'd volunteer to entertain Marti for them. Seemed like a fair exchange.

It was Wednesday, and since I figured there wouldn't be much to do at the cottage, I wanted to stock up on a couple of good books from the library. After Jake dropped me off, I went straight to the front desk. Mrs. Fayerweather was there. When she saw me, she removed her glasses, letting them dangle from a beaded chain around her neck.

Hearing a squeal, I turned to see six small children sitting around a table making a paper chain. It reminded me of when I used to make paper chains with my sisters to hang on our Christmas tree. A young librarian was directing the activity. When she turned I saw Tate, Children's Librarian, on her tag.

"Martha, are you all right?" Mrs. Fayerweather asked, bringing me back to the present. She must have spoken while I was distracted by the children.

"I'm fine. I was just noticing the children and the librarian. I don't remember seeing a group here before."

Mrs. Fayerweather looked in their direction. "They're on a field trip from a nearby day care. We want to acquaint them with the library early. Tate is very good with the youngsters."

"Never too young to start loving books. Isn't that right, Mrs. Fayerweather?" I said.

"Please call me Linda. After all, I call you Martha. Now, what can I do for you today?"

"Do you have anything on the Poconos?" I asked. "I'm getting married next week and…"

Mrs. Fayerweather, ah, Linda, interrupted. "You're getting married? How delightful!"

"Well yes, I guess it is. We're getting married a week from Sunday, Mother's Day to be exact, at Shadows on the Hudson, then we're going on a trip to the Poconos."

"A honeymoon? That's fantastic!" Linda exclaimed without waiting for confirmation.

"Yes, a honeymoon. Our friend is loaning us his cottage on a lake. Anyway, I'd like to read about the area while I'm there. Fiction or nonfiction. Doesn't matter."

Linda started typing away on her computer. She made a few notes on a little pad then said, "Follow me. I have just the ticket."

I followed her to the stacks. In her early sixties, Linda walked more slowly than Winter. Also, unlike Winter, Linda looked like a librarian. Short brown hair, ample hips, black slacks, blue blouse under a cardigan, and sensible shoes similar to mine.

After we walked down a row of books, she stopped, pulled one out and offered it to me, announcing, "*The Bucknoll Cottage Chronicles* by Mary Lowengard." Unlike Winter, who left me to explore the book on my own, Linda read from the back. "Sex In The City meets Under The Tuscan Sun but no sex, no city, and in the Poconos. It's kind of a beach read without a beach."

I took the book from her hand. "No sex, no city, no beach. Sounds a little blah."

Linda frowned. "Well, when you put it that way…"

I stuffed the book in my bag. "I'm sure it will be enlightening. Anything else?"

Linda started walking again. "Since I figured you're not looking for a hiking guide, how about *The Poconos:*

Pennsylvania's Mountain Treasure? You said you wanted to learn about the region." We stopped at the stack featuring guidebooks and she handed the book to me.

"Perfect. I think that will do it. Thanks for your help."

"Any time. I hope you have a marvelous wedding and honeymoon."

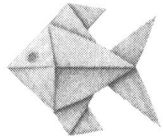

Chapter Thirty-Two

On the ride home from the library, someone in the back of the van was listening to a podcast on their phone—without earbuds. So annoying, but the experience gave me an idea for Harold's wedding gift; earphones that attached to the television so he could watch, but I wouldn't have to listen.

I wasn't sure how the television viewing was going to work after we moved in together. Normally, I watched football, *The Equalizer*, and *Matlock* on my own. Also, my church service. Harold seemed inclined toward basketball, which I found boring, especially now that Michael Jordan was out of the picture.

We'd have to compromise, of course. That's what marriage was all about. Maybe he'd learn to like football and I'd learn to enjoy watching tall men run back and forth across a slippery floor. We both liked movies, so that was something.

I walked in the front door of the Manor and immediately spotted The Mole. She was sitting on her walker seat, hanging around the front desk as if she were waiting for someone. I decided to grab the bull, or rather mole, by the horns.

"Excuse me," I began. "I'm Martha Anderson, an ambassador here at the Manor. I don't believe we've met." I shifted my book bag to my hand holding my purse, then held out my free hand to her.

She stood up, raised the seat of her walker and positioned herself behind the handles. "I know who you are," she said, her eyes narrowed and her chin jutted out. "You're the woman who's a suspect in the murder of Joey Russo."

I ignored this rude statement. I really wanted her name. "And you are?"

"I'm the person who's going to get justice for Joey."

With that, she pointed her walker toward the door, pushed the button for the door to open automatically, and exited the building. I watched as she tottered down the front walk. I didn't see a waiting car. Perhaps the hasty exit was simply to avoid answering further questions.

Stunned, I walked to the elevator. As is often the case when I'm upset, I ended up on the wrong floor and had to backtrack to my apartment. At the moment, all I could think was, *boy, will it be good to get out of here!*

When I finally unlocked my door, I put my book bag on the table, pulled out my journal, and added to my list of when-I-get-back items:

1. Find out who the damn mole is!!

2. I think she's out to get me—maybe working for Agatha

I added a new category to my list. *Description of The Mole.* I was afraid I'd forget what she looked like by the time I returned from our trip. Although I'd seen her at least twice in the cafeteria, it was always from a distance.

1. Old but probably not as old as me

2. Uses a walker but surprisingly nimble

3. Very short, thinning white hair - I could see the pink of her scalp

4. No makeup or jewelry

5. Hanging down boobs - probably doesn't wear a bra

6. Average size - a little stooped but still a few inches taller than me

7. Voice like gravel - smoker?

I felt rattled by recent events. Origami messages times two and The Mole, say nothing of the fact I was about to get married. To keep my focus, once I finished the description of The Mole, I closed the notebook and put it away.

After getting a glass of water, I picked up my laptop and sat in my recliner. I logged into Amazon and after a bit of research, I ordered "Wireless Headphones for TV with Transmitter Charging Base." Included in the description was "Gifts for the Elderly." The gift wasn't at the same spending level as two leather recliners, but it seemed practical, and I thought Harold would appreciate the thoughtfulness.I was tempted to start reading one of the Pocono books, but laid them aside for when I was actually in the region. A honeymoon at our ages seemed a bit ridiculous, but I was looking forward to getting away. Communal, institutional living could get tedious. Even if the meals at the cottage amounted to frozen dinners and PB&J sandwiches, at least it would be a change.

I dressed early for dinner. Then, feeling of sound mind, I texted Harold.

> I'll pick you up tonight. I want to see what's going on with the door.

> Text me if you get turned around. Door looking good!

Harold was right. The door between the studio and his apartment was installed and looked professional. Trim work was needed but it was close to being finished. I strolled into the studio, which had been newly painted a soft gray with bright white floorboards. It felt small but I reminded myself that I would mostly be sleeping in this space. I needed to find a new home for my loveseat. Fond memories were attached to it but there wasn't space and Harold's couch seemed more appropriate for our main living room. Besides, it was super comfy.

On the way to dinner, I told Harold about coming face-to-face with The Mole and her response.

"That pretty much confirms the fact she's an adversary of some sort," Harold said.

"But," I squeezed his arm, "I've put everything aside for now. I even downloaded all my thoughts into a notebook so my mind will be free from what you call investigative mode for the next two weeks."

Harold patted my hand that was hooked into his elbow. "Thanks."

The next day, both Ethyl and Laura were missing from our table of four.

"Where are the others?" Sue asked after we settled into our seats.

"I don't know. I haven't heard from either of them," I replied, stirring my bowl of beef stew.

"I hope they're all right."

Frankly, I was also worried about Sue. Although she had her portable oxygen tank by her side, her breathing was labored and she looked pale.

"How are you?" I asked.

Her lips went up but the slight smile didn't reach her eyes. "I'll be okay. Just not a particularly good day." She paused for a breath. "Hard to catch my breath sometimes." Sue looked toward the door for our friends. "Why don't you text Laura and Ethyl. Ask them if they're coming. Perhaps they're just a little late."

I texted them both but had no response. Not even a thumbs up. "I'll stop by Ethyl's apartment after lunch. Laura frequently takes a nap, so perhaps she'll check in later."

I too looked toward the door but I was watching for The Mole. Even though I'd tucked her away in my notebook for later consideration, I couldn't help but monitor her whereabouts.

As promised, I stopped by Ethyl's apartment after lunch. There was no response when I knocked, so I knocked harder.

A loud voice said, "Go away and leave me alone."

"Ethyl, it's Martha. Let me in."

"Go away. I'm in no mood for visitors."

"That's exactly why you need to let me in," I stubbornly insisted.

"Come back later."

"Okay," I said, "but know that I care about you. Call me if you need anything."

In a voice so soft I could barely hear her through the door, Ethyl responded. "I will."

I returned to my apartment and settled into my recliner to read. I set the alarm on my phone for two hours. I didn't want to forget to check on Ethyl as promised.

When I knocked on her door at three o'clock, she responded in a faint voice. "Door's open."

Ethyl's living room reminded me of my old friend Madge's apartment. She, too, was depressed but used alcohol to keep her going.

The drapes were pulled and the room was dark. The walls were beige, the two overstuffed chairs were a brown tweed, and the braided area rug was stained. Ethyl looked haggard.

"Have a seat," she said, gesturing toward the other chair. "Want a soda?"

"No thanks."

I sat in the offered chair. "What's going on? We missed you at lunch."

Ethyl squinted in my direction. "It's the Lamictal."

"Your medication?"

"Yes. It has side effects. My doctor recently increased my dose. Blurry vision, nausea…" she held out her arm, "skin rash."

I leaned forward to look at the rash. "Looks nasty."

"Nothing serious but annoying."

I knew I needed to tread carefully. Ethyl was super sensitive. "Once you adjust to the new dose, will you feel better?"

"I hope so."

"Me too. You know…" I smiled at Ethyl, "You have a wedding to go to."

"Would you be disappointed if I didn't go?" Ethyl asked in a small, almost childlike voice.

"I would. It's not every day someone makes a friend out of a sworn enemy."

For the first time, Ethyl straightened up in her chair and looked in my direction. "I don't have anything to wear."

I pointed toward her bedroom. "Let's take a look. I bet I can uncover something that will be just right."

Ethyl got up slowly, putting her hand on a nearby table to steady herself. After she stood for a moment, she led the way to her bedroom closet. Surprisingly, her bed was made, covered in a green chenille bedspread.

We stood in front of her closet for a beat before I noticed a navy blue shirtwaist dress shoved toward the back. I pulled it out. "Does this fit you?"

"My weight's been the same for years."

"Lucky you."

"But that dress is so boring. I'd look like a librarian. Not Winter, of course." When a small smile crossed Ethyl's lips, I felt encouraged that she was coming out of her depression.

"It's all about the accessories. Do you order from Amazon?"

"Who doesn't?" Ethyl pulled out her phone and clicked on the app.

"Order red earrings, a red pashmina, and red sandals," I instructed.

Ethyl's finger paused over her phone. "What's a pashmina?"

"It's a light-weight shawl. Perfect for wearing to an outdoor spring wedding."

I trailed her back to the living room, where she continued searching. She brought her phone over to show me her order. "Good?"

"Perfect." I walked over to the curtains and drew them back, letting in the afternoon sun. "Hungry?"

"No. But I do think my nausea is getting better."

"Want me to bring you dinner later?"

"I'll go down."

"Promise?"

"Promise." Ethyl turned her head towards me. "By the way, you're the first person other than staff to visit me in my apartment. Do you think it needs some accessorizing too?"

I looked around the room. "Add a couple of bright colored throw pillows and a matching area rug to your order. The maintenance guys will help you dispose of your old one."

Ethyl picked up her phone and thumbed the keys. "How about orange?"

"Orange will do as long as it's a color you love."

"Done."

I got up and went to the door. "See you at lunch tomorrow."

Ethyl nodded. "Thanks, Martha. You really are the friend I never had."

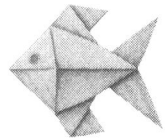

Chapter Thirty-Three

The whole Bizzy Buddies crew was at lunch the next day. Turns out Laura had slept through lunch the day before. She was her jovial self but seemed extra frail. Sue's breathing was better, but Ethyl still looked drawn and pale.

"Anything new on the…" Sue looked around at the people near our table, "case?" she whispered.

I told them about Kathleen also receiving an origami with a message and that I'd figured out both were from Agatha. I also told them about my encounter with The Mole.

When I described her, Laura spoke up. "That sounds like Mabel McAllister. I met her at Bingo last week." Laura looked over at me. "She even asked how I knew you."

"Me? Why?"

"She didn't say. I told her we met when you introduced yourself as a Manor Ambassador."

Sue leaned in, "I'll find out who she is. Leave it to me." She sat up straight and looked around the table. "I love being in this group!"

The next day, we assembled with Cobb salads in front of us, except Ethyl, who was having chicken noodle soup. I figured her stomach was probably still upset. Sue unzipped her crossbody purse and pulled out a scrap of paper. "My assignment is complete," she announced.

"Tell us," Laura said.

"Well, Mabel McAllister, aka The Mole, is from Brooklyn, as was our recently deceased resident, Joey Russo, his ex-wife, Rosa, and bearded-guy, Ralph Jensen." Sue looked at me. "Did I miss anyone?"

"Joey's son, JD, and Agatha, the redhead."

"Oh, yes," Sue acknowledged. "It's difficult keeping track of all the characters. Anyway, Mabel can very well be a relative of Agatha's. They lived in the same neighborhood in Brooklyn and came to the Manor about the same time. Of course, Agatha has since moved out, but I'm guessing she still communicates with Mabel on a regular basis. They go way back."

Ethyl perked up at this and asked, "Do you think Mabel could have known Joey back in the day? Perhaps an old boyfriend?"

"Possibly. Their ages match up. Although Joey was from a different neighborhood, their paths could have crossed in church or at work," Sue answered.

"Church? You think Joey went to church?" Laura asked.

"Most Italian kids go to church at some stage of their lives. First communion, confirmation, and all that. Joey and Mabel could have been in the same parish."

I tried to put the pieces together. "So, both Agatha and Mabel came to the Manor because of Russo and probably knew him from when they lived in Brooklyn. Now that Agatha is banned from the place, Mabel has picked up the investigation into Russo's stash. Since Agatha still thinks I know where it is, she's put Mabel on my tail. Is that about it?"

"You got it, Martha," Sue confirmed. "Now here's an idea." She looked around the table and lowered her voice. "Even though Mabel has seen me sitting with you all at lunch, I thought I'd try to befriend her while Martha's away on her honeymoon. Maybe she'll think the group has broken up."

"It's worth a try," said Laura. "Maybe you can confirm whether or not she was the person who delivered the origami to Martha."

Sue looked at me. "In the meantime, I hope you can set all this aside and enjoy your time away."

"I intend to do just that. But, just to let you guys know, I've made a list of all the questions we're trying to get answers to so that when I return, I can jump right back into the game."

"Will it be all right if Laura and I continue to lunch together?" asked Ethyl in a small voice.

Laura spoke up. "Of course! While the other two are out on assignment, you and I will keep the home fires burning."

Ethyl smiled for the first time since we'd sat down for lunch. I could tell she was relieved to know she'd have a reason to leave her apartment.

Chapter Thirty-Four

It was the week before the wedding. Bobbie and Barbara were arriving on Friday night, so they'd have all day Saturday to help me pack for the honeymoon and the move to my new apartment. My daughters were arriving later Saturday but staying at a hotel. I wouldn't see Richard's family until the day of the wedding.

Harold's daughter, Jennifer, son, John, granddaughter, Sarah, and great- granddaughter, Marcella all lived nearby. His once wayward son was bringing a plus-one. For Harold's sake, I hoped he'd cleaned up his act.

—

On Saturday morning, when I laid eyes on Marti, I couldn't believe how much she'd grown. She was in a front pack attached to my granddaughter. Bobbi was close behind, lugging a bulging denim diaper bag. After Marti was removed from her pouch and there were hugs all around, Barbara said, "Let's get to work."

By lunch, the girls had packed my bag for the Poconos and emptied my few cupboards and drawers into cardboard boxes.

We decided to carry my clothes to my new closet on hangers. They made a neat stack of what I'd wear the following day.

"Are you ready for the big day?" Bobbi asked while we were walking to lunch.

"As ready as I'll ever be," I replied.

When we were finally seated in the dining room, Barbara spooned some mashed carrots into Marti's mouth, then turned toward me. "Uncle Richard told Mom there was a murder here a while back."

I kept my response brief. "Maybe a murder, but more likely a suicide."

"Uncle Richard was pretty convinced it was murder. Apparently, he was launching a campaign to get you to move to a new location. Guess that didn't work out. I don't think moving up a floor counts."

"I told him in no uncertain terms that I didn't want to move. This is my home. I have friends and a life here. He uprooted me once, but I'm not letting him do it again."

"Seems to me that first uprooting has led to something good," Bobbi interjected. "Here you are—getting married!"

"Yes, here I am getting married. Do you think I'm a foolish old lady?"

In turn, each girl replied that they didn't think I was a fool. They looked so earnest that I believed them.

Barbara moved on. "Let's just the three of us go someplace fun tonight. It'll be your bachelorette party. Mom said she'll arrive in time to come over and watch Marti. We'll get you back early. What do you say?"

I thought for a moment. Was I up to going out the night before my wedding?

"I can't pass up an offer like that. Do you have a place in mind?"

The girls looked at each other. "We hoped you'd ask," Barbara replied. "We'd suggest the Mill House Brewing Company. It's located in a rehabilitated mill and the food is locally sourced. We know you like beer, Gram."

"Sounds perfect. When we get back to my apartment, lay out something for me to wear, then pick me up at five-thirty. Now, let's finish lunch so I can rest up for my" I chucked to myself, "first and only bachelorette party."

Like me, Marti was ready to move on, pushing away a last spoonful of something green.

—

As promised, the girls arrived at my door on time. We all wore jeans, mine skinny and pull-on, theirs holey and faded. They had rented a car so we walked together to the parking lot.

The front of the brewery was a combination of brick and clapboard. There was a second-floor outdoor terrace, a three-story attached building, and a garage turned into additional dining space. It was a very interesting place.

We opted to eat indoors. It was a pleasant evening, but cool. The girls fussed over me. "We don't want to be responsible for you catching a cold just before your honeymoon," Bobbi said.

Unfortunately, the maître d' overheard her. "Ahh, are we celebrating a future bride tonight?" he asked, looking from one girl to the other.

"Yes, my grandmother is getting married tomorrow. This is her bachelorette party," Barbara replied. She smiled when he looked at her in disbelief. "Don't you think she'll make a lovely bride?"

Apparently trying to regain his composure, he stuttered, "Of, of course. I'll ask your server to comp you a dessert." With that, he whisked us away to a table in the corner.

The appetizer selection was so tempting, we decided to order several and take a pass on ordering main courses. One of their classic offerings was fried pickle chips which sounded interesting. I added them to our order.

When our server, a college lad with long blonde hair and a mustache, came to take our order, I asked for a lite beer. He frowned. "We only serve wine and cocktails."

"But you're a brewery," Bobbi said.

"We took the name only. We do have a lovely wine selection."

The girls looked at the menu. "How about a bottle of Tullia Prosecco?" Barbara suggested. "How does that sound, Gram?"

"Perfect. More celebratory than beer."

The Saturday night crowd had shuffled in and the noise level was high. Other than that, the atmosphere was pleasant with a modern, industrial look. They definitely had… what was it? Oh yes, rehabilitated the place.

We drank our bubbly, the girls toasting my marriage, then we passed around the three fish tacos, tikka masala meatballs, bang bang cauliflower, and the fried pickle chips with sriracha ranch. For dessert, the server brought a complimentary dark chocolate flourless cake with chocolate glaze and candied orange peel, accompanied by three forks.

Per my request, the girls had me back to my apartment by eight-thirty. Even though I was tired, I tossed and turned thinking about what lay ahead. The wedding, the honeymoon, a new apartment. I pushed to the side all the potential thoughts about the Russo Case.

I was awakened in the night, however, by a dream of Joey tossing his own apartment and putting a pinch of something in a drink. It seemed so real that when I awoke in the morning, I had to reorient myself around the fact that it was a dream and not the actual event.

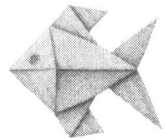

Chapter Thirty-Five

The girls came by at eight-thirty with toast and tea, insisting that I eat something prior to the wedding and brunch. I was in my kimono when they arrived, my fancy dress laid out on the bed, and my suitcase open on the floor awaiting the last minute inclusion of cosmetics.

Marti was adorable in her navy blue and white sailor suit. She'd grown some hair since I'd last seen her, and she had a red bow attached to her head. The girls had on spring dresses. Barbara's was a tailored shirtwaist not unlike Ethyl's; Bobbi wore a flowery number.

Laura, Ethyl, and Sue, along with Harold's friends, were going to the wedding in the minivan. Even though it was Jake's usual day off, he'd agreed to take them and bring them back.

"Anything for you, Mrs. A," Jake said when I asked him about driving.

"It's going to be Mrs. L the next time you see me."

"Remind me if I forget."

—

At nine-fifteen, Barbara and I walked to the front door. Bobbi had pulled the rental car up to the curb and I joined Marti, who was in her car seat, in the back. I couldn't have asked for a more perfect day. The sun was shining, there was a light breeze, and the sky was clear without a raincloud in sight.

—

Shadows on the Hudson lived up to its reputation as a charming waterfront restaurant. Sitting on a cliff above the Hudson River, the restaurant offered a stunning view of green hillsides and a lovely trestle bridge. Our private dining room overlooked the river. A sweet bouquet of pink roses and white daisies with baby's breath, per Harold's request, sat on each of four round tables set for our twenty-seven guests.

There was a mini bar on the side with pink, personalized cocktail napkins in a neat fan near the glassware. After the ceremony, each guest would go through the brunch buffet line which had everything anyone could want, including a carving station. Potted red tulips and yellow daffodils marched down the center of the serving tables.

French doors led from our private room onto the veranda, which thankfully, was shaded. An arch festooned with spring flowers sat in front of the railing which faced the river. Since the service would be brief, we'd only requested a few chairs, primarily for our friends from the Manor.

After I determined all was well with the room and veranda, my daughters whisked me to the lounge in the ladies' bathroom so I'd remain unseen until my appearance up the aisle. It seemed a bit much, but I went along for the ride.

Ruth was the lookout. When she determined that everyone was in their proper places, she and Elizabeth escorted me back to the terrace. I clutched the five white roses Elizabeth handed me and straightened my lavender lace dress. I was as ready as I'd ever be.

The restaurant provided a recording of the wedding march. When it began, Marcella solemnly walked down the aisle tossing pink rose petals as she went. Adorable in her pink dress with fluttery sleeves, she proudly positioned herself beside her GiGi, who looked nervous but handsome in his black suit and shiny shoes. His tie, gray with subdued lavender stripes, nearly matched my dress. Apparently, there was more than one mole in my life.

Sue, with her oxygen tank by her side, looked very official in a white robe. She smiled at my approach, which eased some of my tension.

I bravely proceeded up the short aisle and took my place next to Harold, who immediately took my ice-cold hand in his. Why was I so nervous? Worst case scenario, this marriage would only last a few years. Best case, I'd end my life with a loving companion. I was betting on the latter.

My attention returned to the ceremony. "Martha Anderson, do you take Harold Lancaster to be your lawfully wedded husband, to have and to hold, from this day forward, for better, for worse, for richer, for poorer, in sickness and in health, until death do you part?"

"I do."

Harold acknowledged his vow, then Marcella handed him the little pouch with our rings. He placed a ring on my finger, and I put one on his.

Sue opened her arms toward us and said, "I pronounce you husband and wife. You may kiss the bride."

Harold leaned down and kissed me, then we turned to face our guests, who applauded their congratulations. We walked together up the aisle and back through the French doors to the dining room with Marcella following in our wake.

Someone took my roses, Susan handed us glasses of champagne, and we toasted. "To us," Harold said.

"We really did it," I added.

When I set my champagne glass on the table, my eyes were drawn to my old-lady hands. Tendons stood out alongside raised blue veins. Two fingers on my right hand, the ones I'd closed in a car door as a child, were crooked with arthritis. The new diamond on my left ring finger glistened in the sunlight. The tiny diamond in the ring on my right hand pinky finger also glowed as if Missy was smiling at me from above.

—

The oldest and youngest soon bonded. Bobbi took Marti to meet my friends and she was passed from lap to lap, smiling and gurgling at each old lady in turn. When Barbara approached, I overheard her complimenting Ethyl on her outfit. Little did my granddaughter know what a difference her gesture made. Funny how life works. It's often the small, unplanned words that create the most lasting impact.

Harold's son John and his companion, Jackie, were speaking with my grandson Rich and his wife, Samantha. John, who once lived in a ramshackle house and harbored his father against his will, looked very respectable in an open-collared shirt and sports jacket. His plus-one was a plain woman with gray hair pulled back into a French twist. Dressed in an unflattering skirt and blouse, she was, however, engaged in an animated discussion with Rich while John looked on, hanging on her every word.

For some odd reason, Steve Billings popped into my mind just as I was enjoying my medium-rare roast beef. The subject of Harold's and my Purse Snatcher Case, Steve had served his time in prison and had become our friend. We hadn't seen him for a while, and I wondered what he was up to. I made a mental note to send him a photo from the wedding.

By the time the festivities drew to a close, I was physically and mentally exhausted. Harold had arranged for John and Jackie to take us back to the Manor. I felt bad that I wasn't spending more time with my daughters, but they assured me they needed to return to Chicago and not to worry about them.

"Enjoy your honeymoon, Mom," Ruth said.

"Thanks for coming. It was wonderful to see the family together. Nice that it was a wedding and not a funeral, don't you think?" I replied.

Always the realist, Elizabeth answered. "Who would have guessed?"

I looked from one of my single girls to the other. "It's never too late, you know. Our next gathering could be for one of your weddings."

Without commenting, they both hugged me and said goodbye.

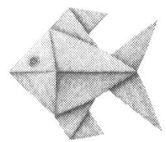

Chapter Thirty-Six

When I awoke the next morning, I hardly recognized my apartment. All of my personal items had been removed, including my clothing. My "traveling outfit," as the girls called it, was laid out on a chair, so I quickly dressed and made my way to breakfast. After eating my Grape Nuts with red raspberries and green tea, I texted Harold.

> Just finished breakfast. I'm ready when you are.

> I'll come by in an hour to get your suitcase. Jennifer is picking us up at ten.

I put my cosmetics in my suitcase and zipped it up, then sat down in my recliner. Josh, the new maintenance man, promised to move it along with my bed, table, and chairs to the studio while we were away. I'd return to a new apartment.

—

Harold's daughter, Jennifer, was a good driver who concentrated on the road. There was little chit-chat and certainly no phones involved. I'd offered to sit in the back so father and daughter could talk but always the gentleman, Harold declined. "You'll be more comfortable up front."

I must have dozed off for a while because it seemed like we were suddenly off the highway and traveling down a street dotted with charming houses.

I hadn't pictured the cottage to be so big or so lovely. The red cedar siding stood out against two large elm trees. Three dormer windows peaked out of the roof facing the street. A wraparound porch with two wooden rocking chairs beckoned guests to sit and ponder the great outdoors.

The temperature was in the mid-60s with the sun occasionally sliding out from behind the clouds. I had my old trench coat on over my skinny jeans and a blue sweater, so I was comfortable. It seemed strange to be away from the Manor and out of the state of New York. In fact, I felt as though I'd been transported to Ireland or some other country with quaint cottages and lovely views.

After unloading our suitcases, Jennifer and Harold carried several bags of groceries into the house while I put them away.

"Thank you," I said to Jennifer when we'd finished. "We'll eat like royalty with minimal cooking."

"That's the plan," she replied. "I even added your chunky peanut butter and Ritz crackers."

"Plus wine for me and beer for you, Mrs. Lancaster," Harold added.

Hearing my new name sent a shiver up my spine. Harold must have noticed because he said, "You'll get used to it."

"I'm going to leave you two to settle in. Call if you need anything. Sarah will pick you up on Sunday right after lunch." After hugging each of us, Jennifer was out the door, and we were left alone in a house where we didn't know where the light switches were located.

"Let's have lunch," I suggested.

After eating chicken salad sandwiches and coleslaw, we spent a leisurely afternoon each absorbed in our own activities. I sat in an old-style, green plaid recliner in the living room and read about the Poconos while Harold puttered around in the garage.

My eyes grew tired and I took a break to survey the room. The focal point was a red brick, wood-burning fireplace with a live-edge mantle. It gave off the delightful, unmistakable scent of past fires. I made an effort to push away a vision of Bob and Audrey sitting before a romantic fire in this room.

My original Irish vibe ran true of the furnishings. Besides the plaid recliner, there were two love seats in the same material, a large coffee table, various end tables, and a wooden rocker with a dark green corduroy cushion. The wall behind the fireplace was cedar paneled, the other walls were painted a light yellow, giving the room a sunshiny hue even when clouds floated across the sun.

When Harold reappeared in the late afternoon, I prepared a tray of olives, cheese, and crackers. Harold uncorked the wine, opened a bottle of beer, and poured our drinks into glasses he found in the cupboard.

"Let's sit on the back deck," Harold suggested. When we stepped outside, the breeze was singing through the trees, and we could see the lake's gentle waves flowing over a gravelly shoreline.

We waved at boaters passing by and our greeting was returned along with broad smiles. "Do you think Bob's neighbors know we're here on our honeymoon?" I asked Harold.

He shrugged his shoulders. "Maybe. They probably aren't accustomed to seeing anyone sitting on this porch. It's been a while since Bob visited."

The cool evening air finally drove us inside. Jennifer had left a prepared dinner in the refrigerator to defrost. It wasn't a Swanson or Marie Callender meal; it was prepared by Sebastian, a private Italian chef. I wondered how she knew I loved Veal Osso Bucco. I whipped up a simple green salad and we sat down to a lovely meal at a table overlooking a pink and orange sky reflected in the lake.

"What a beautiful place. Thanks for making this happen," I said.

"Not bad. Nice to get away from the Manor for a while."

Both of our suitcases were in the downstairs bedroom, so not long after we cleaned up our dinner dishes, tidied up the kitchen, and watched a Matlock rerun, we decided to call it a day and sleep together in the king-sized bed. "I'll move upstairs tomorrow night if either of us doesn't sleep well," Harold promised.

Exhausted from two busy days, we went to bed around nine o'clock. Harold secured the doors and turned off all the lights except for a nightlight in the ensuite bathroom.

When I was awakened by a light coming on in the living room, I looked at the time on my phone—11:00 pm. I wondered if a timer was set to turn on the lights. Just as

I was considering whether or not to wake Harold, I heard footsteps on the stairs. Someone was in the house! And I thought I was done with intruders.

Harold was sound asleep with his lips parted, his eyes buttoned up, and one hand under his cheek. I hated to wake him, but my instincts and my ears had distinctly told me a person had entered the cottage and gone upstairs. Although I was alarmed by the notion that a stranger was in our domain, I felt surprisingly calm knowing Harold was asleep beside me. He was no longer a Colonel in the Army, but I knew he still had the instincts of a soldier and not just any soldier, but a commander.

"Harold, wake up," I whispered.

When he opened his eyes, he seemed surprised to see me. "Martha?"

"Someone's upstairs."

Harold sat up and gave his head a little shake. "What?"

"I saw a light come on in the living room, then I heard someone going upstairs."

"Who?"

Obviously, Harold had yet to become fully engaged with the world.

Patiently and slowly I reiterated. "Two minutes ago, I saw the living room light come on. Then…" I looked to be sure Harold was tracking.

"Go on. I'm with you."

"Then I heard someone walking up the stairs. When they reached the top, the living room light went out and a light went on in the hallway at the top of the stairs. See?" I pointed toward our open bedroom door.

"There's a light on at the top of the stairs."

Growing impatient yet trying to keep my voice low, I said, "That's what I just said. Should we call the police?"

"But I turned off all the lights."

"I know you did. Do you think we should call the police?" I repeated.

Harold swung his legs over the side of the bed, retrieved the sweatpants he'd worn earlier, pulled them on, and then headed toward the door. "I'll go check."

"What if the intruder has a weapon?" I asked beginning to feel alarmed.

"If I don't show aggression, I doubt if they'll shoot me." He turned toward the bed. "You wait here. If I'm not back in a few minutes, call the police."

"I don't like this," I stated.

"Duly noted."

I got out of bed, put my kimono on, and walked as far as the bedroom door. From there, I watched Harold slowly and quietly climb the carpeted stairs. My phone was in my hand, ready to punch in 911 if necessary.

When he reached the top of the stairs, Harold shouted, "Audrey, what the hell are you doing here?" Then, "Martha, it's all right. It's just Audrey."

I didn't want to miss out on all the excitement so with that pronouncement, I quickly proceeded up the stairs.

Audrey, still in her jeans and sweatshirt, her hair in disarray, looked like the Cheshire Cat, the one with the mischievous grin in *Alice in Wonderland*. "What are YOU doing here?" she retorted, hands on her hips like she wasn't just caught breaking and entering.

"Martha and I are here on our honeymoon as guests of Bob Bell. You remember Bob, don't you?" Harold asked sarcastically. "The person who owns this place? The person you hoodwinked."

Harold wasn't fooling around.

"Your honeymoon!" Audrey said in a voice much louder than necessary.

"That's all you've got?" I asked her.

"Why we're here isn't the point," Harold admonished her. "You're trespassing and if you don't leave immediately, Martha," he pointed at me, and I dutifully held up my phone, "is going to call the police."

Still trying to stay in control, Audrey turned on her heel. "Well, if that's the way you're going to be, I'll gather my things and move on."

"You just do that," Harold said as he followed her into the bedroom where a suitcase lay open on the bed.

Audrey slammed her suitcase closed, zipped it up, and yanked it off the bed. Then she hurried down the stairs with Harold and me close behind.

She opened the front door, walked to a car parked in the driveway, and threw her suitcase into the trunk. After she sped away, Harold closed the door and we stood motionless for a few beats.

"Good grief!" I said loud enough for the neighbors to hear if we had neighbors. "What just happened?"

"I imagine she made a copy of the key before she handed over the originals to Bob after she'd taken over the place a few years ago. Now she treats it as her personal retreat. She certainly showed no remorse for being caught red-handed."

I was getting cold. "Let's discuss this under the covers." I walked to the bedroom, and Harold followed. After we were cozy in our big bed, I said, "What next?"

"I'll call Bob in the morning and let him know what happened. I'll ask him if he wants me to arrange for a locksmith to come and change the locks while we're here. I doubt if he'll want to take any kind of legal action against Audrey."

Harold took my hand. I could tell he somehow felt responsible. "I'm sorry this happened on our first night here."

"You had no idea Audrey was going to show up. A little excitement in the middle of the night isn't the end of the world."

Harold looked over at the clock. "It's only eleven thirty, hardly the middle of the night, but I'm happy to know I'm married to a woman who's willing to roll with the punches and not complain." He looked closely at me. "Knowing you, this was just another adventure to add to your long list of escapades."

I smiled. Harold knew me so well.

"Now, My Knight In Shining Armor, it's time to go back to sleep. I promise not to wake you again unless…" I squeezed Harold's arm, "There's another intruder."

Harold kissed me, then slid down into the covers. "Good night, Mrs. Lancaster. Sweet dreams."

Chapter Thirty-Seven

The next three days were peaceful. A fire in the fireplace kept us snug during the cool evenings, and afternoon walks acquainted us with the neighborhood.

The locksmith came on Wednesday to change the locks. He gave us extra keys to take back to Bob. He was a local guy with a lot of questions. Harold answered discreetly, not wanting to embarrass Bob.

Friday dawned sunny and warm without a cloud in the sky. I made scrambled eggs and toast for breakfast, burning neither the frying pan nor the eggs.

Since the morning was especially inviting, we decided to get our exercise early. I walked out the front door and smelled the warming earth and the blossoming cherry tree growing on the side of the house. There were no sidewalks, so we carefully walked along the side of the road, which was surfaced with a packed down mixture of oil and gravel.

Hearing a car coming from behind, I stepped in front of Harold to make way. Just as the car went by, I took a step, then lost my balance on a dip in the road. I suddenly found myself lying on my right side on the ground.

Harold immediately dropped to his knees to see if I was hurt. The driver of the passing car pulled over and stopped to offer assistance.

"Are you all right?" Harold asked with concern written all over his face.

"I think I broke my arm," I squeaked out, trying not to cry. My arm really hurt and I was worried that I might have done more damage that I didn't know about. I pointed, "Maybe you and that gentleman can help me up. Just don't touch my right arm."

After they got me up and standing on wobbly legs, the neighbor introduced himself.

"I'm Joe Weaver from down the street. I'd be glad to take you to the nearest emergency clinic to get that arm checked out."

Harold held out his hand. "We're Martha and Harold Lancaster, and we'd be much obliged for your assistance. We're here without transportation until Sunday."

"Don't worry. I'll get you to where you need to go." Joe turned to me. "Let me help you into the car, Mrs. Lancaster."

"Please call me Martha."

After I was settled in the front seat with Harold in the back, Joe turned the car around and headed away from the lake. I cradled my right arm with my left. It hurt like hell, especially when we hit a bump in the road.

I guessed that Joe was a little younger than my son, probably around sixty-five. When I asked if he was retired, he said, "Turned my construction company over to the son last year, then me and the wife moved up here to our lake house full-time."

"Do you know Bob Bell?" Harold asked.

"I've heard of him but we've never met. Are you staying in his cottage?"

"We are," Harold said. "Bob offered it to us for our honeymoon."

A smile crept over Joe's long, unshaven face. "Congratulations. This certainly isn't good timing for a fall."

Joe had a gray baseball cap on that said Fishaholic across the front. He had the slow drawl of a guy patient enough to spend the day waiting for a fish to bite or an old lady to get a broken arm taken care of.

I looked out the car window to distract myself from the pain. Bright new leaves on sugar maple and dogwood trees glistened in the breeze. A woman was walking her shaggy dog. Some houses weren't more than small fishing cottages, others were grand with ornate landscaping, double front doors, and three-car garages.

After a twenty-minute drive, which felt like sixty, we finally arrived at Lake Region Urgent Care on Spruce Street in Hawley. Joe ran into the building and returned with a wheelchair.

"That's not necessary," I said, easing myself out of the car.

Harold stepped up and said in a kind but no-nonsense voice, "Sit down, Martha."

After I sat down, he wheeled me in while Joe parked the car.

I was thoroughly examined by an elderly doctor. Perhaps this was his retirement gig. He pronounced me sound, other than the arm. "The X-ray showed a simple break. The bones are in position, so there's no surgery required," he said. "The nurse will be in shortly to apply a plaster cast." Harold sat nearby through it all.

"Take it easy for a few days, Mrs. Lancaster," Dr. Morgan said when my arm was in a cast and there was a sling around my neck. "The fall undoubtedly caused some trauma to your body. Don't be surprised if you're stiff and sore tomorrow." He looked at Harold. "I'm sure you'll take good care of this young lady."

"I certainly will," said Harold. "What can she take for pain?"

"I'll give you some Tylenol samples. She can take them as needed according to the directions."

We left the examining room and found Joe slouched down in a chair waiting for us. "All set?" he asked, eyeing my cast.

"We can't thank you enough for getting us here," I said to Joe while he wheeled me out to his parked car.

With my arm stabilized and a Tylenol in my system, the ride home was more comfortable. Joe dropped us off in our driveway, and Harold shook his hand. "Thanks again. Without your assistance I would have had to call 911."

"Just bein' a good neighbor. You folks have a restful day."

After I was propped up in a comfortable chair with a cup of hot tea by my side, Harold sat down across from me. "We should have stayed in our safe assisted living apartments."

I thought he was about to cry.

"This is all my fault."

"Oh, for heaven's sake, Harold, don't be ridiculous. As you well know, a fall can happen any time, any place. I don't regret coming here for a minute. It's been a delightful week." I took a sip of my tea to end the conversation. "Now go look in the refrigerator and figure out what we're having for lunch."

That afternoon, we found Rummikub in the console under the television and entertained ourselves with a game that required only one hand. I dutifully kept my arm in the sling, which gave me a sore neck but I was grateful I hadn't broken a hip or something else that would have put me in the hospital.

Knowing we needed to have full disclosure (it was hard to hide a cast), we sent text messages to our families assuring them that I had been well cared for by the local physician and Harold was an excellent nurse. Sarah offered to pick us up a day early, but we declined.

"Are you sure you don't want to get back right away?" Harold asked.

"I'm sure. You're just going to have to play nurse, chief cook and bottle washer for another day."

—

Our honeymoon turned out to be a more intimate affair than I'd anticipated. Saturday morning, Harold figured out a way to cover my cast with a plastic garbage bag so I could shower, but I needed his help with drying off and dressing.

"Bet you'll be glad when you can turn your nursing duties over to Judy," I said after thanking him for buttoning up my blouse (I gave up on either of us trying to put on a bra).

"You mean you're going to fire me as your nurse when we get back to the Manor? I kinda like the perks," Harold replied with a mischievous grin.

As planned, Harold's granddaughter Sarah picked us up after lunch on Sunday. Sitting alone in the back seat of the car, I had time to reminisce about our week in the Poconos. Experiencing Harold's gentle kindness and patience, I felt like my love for him had deepened.

I also realized that even though I resided in assisted living, knowing I had a partner who was willing and able to take care of me through thick and thin was priceless. Being together 24 hours a day and under some unusual circumstances (to say the least), the bond between us grew, and I was grateful to return to the Manor and my new apartment as Mrs. Lancaster.

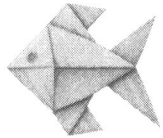

Chapter Thirty-Eight

The Bizzy Buddies were together again at lunch on Monday. Upon seeing my cast, Ethyl asked, "What did you do now?" The question lacked empathy but I smiled, thinking of how much Ethyl reminded me of my old friend Madge, who was equally outspoken.

"I tripped and fell while out walking," I explained.

"Besides the broken arm, how was your time away?" asked Laura, a naturally kinder soul.

"It was lovely. Cozy cottage surrounded by breathtaking scenery. We had appetizers while sitting on a deck facing the lake, enjoyed evenings in front of a fire, and generally appreciated each other's company." I smiled at my friends, glad to be back with them. "Enough about me, tell me what's been happening around here."

The others looked to Sue, who'd been tasked with finding out about Mabel The Mole, and she reported in. The serious tone of her voice gave her extra credibility. "Mabel's the mole all right. Probably going back to when Russo was alive. Joey's sister is an old friend of hers."

Ethyl interrupted with a question. "I'm one of the originals here and it's only recently that I've seen her on a regular basis. Do you know how long she's lived here?"

Showing no frustration over being interrupted, Sue continued her report. "I wasn't able to ascertain when she moved in, but I think she's been living here a while. Longer than we first thought. She makes an effort to keep a low profile."

"Do you think she delivered the box with the origami to Martha's apartment?" Laura asked.

"She didn't admit to it, but I could see guilt written all over her face when I asked her about it. Also, Mabel blames Martha for everything bad that happened to Russo, going all the way back to when he was arrested for setting off fire alarms and breaking into her apartment. She was eager to relate the stories to me."

It was my turn to ask a question. "Do you think she knows anything about Russo's supposed stash?"

"What stash?" Sue asked.

"People from Joey's past believe he was involved in a bank heist years ago and stashed away money or valuables. This, quote stash, could be a motive for his murder. IF, and I mean IF, he was murdered, which I'm beginning to doubt," I explained.

Ethyl spoke up again. "So do we add Mabel The Mole to our list of suspects?"

"I think so," offered Sue. "She's angry, and she has a bad attitude toward Martha. Kinda makes you wonder why, doesn't it?"

"Sure does," Ethyl said. "You can't shovel shit and call it sugar."

When three heads turned and looked at her, Ethyl shrugged her shoulders. "Something my pa used to say. Seemed to fit here. You know, it's like Mabel saying bad things about Martha and us not thinking she has bad intentions. It certainly isn't sugar she's shoveling."

I couldn't help but chuckle. "That's a dadism for sure. I have a whole raft of them."

"What's your favorite?" asked Laura.

I thought for a moment. "When something was really cool, my dad used to say, 'That's slicker than snot on a doorknob.'" Laura seemed to make a mental note, and I asked, "Planning on using it in a story?"

"It's definitely a saying I've never heard. Can't think of how I'd work it in, but you never know." Laura looked over at Ethyl. "May I use your dad's saying if I have an opportunity?"

"I'd be honored," Ethyl replied.

"Boy, aren't we literary today," offered Sue. "Now, getting back to the case, what's next?"

I skootched my chair out. Getting up one-armed was challenging. "Let me get my feet back on the ground, then I'll give Detective Niles a call and see where they are at their end." I straightened my sling. "See you all tomorrow. It's good to be back."

"It's good to have you back," Laura said. The others nodded their agreement.

—

That afternoon, I called the precinct. My call was directed to Detective Niles. "Detective Warren has taken an early retirement," she explained when I asked about him.

"That was rather abrupt," I said.

"We all thought so too," Niles confided in a soft voice. "The opinion around here is that he got bored working the desk where he was assigned after returning from administrative leave."

"So, he just up and retired?"

There was silence on the other end then Niles said, "Word has it that he left his wife and moved to Vietnam."

I was completely taken aback. "Vietnam?"

"Apparently, his father was stationed in Saigon during the war. He found out there was a possibility that he has step-siblings still living there, and he wanted to find them."

"So, what's happened to the Russo case?" I asked. "Are you now in charge?"

"The case is closed. There wasn't enough evidence to show he was murdered, so it's assumed he committed suicide. You're off the hook, Mrs. Anderson."

"It's Mrs. Lancaster now," I said.

"Congratulations. Now, if there's nothing else, I need to get back to work."

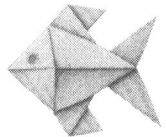

Chapter Thirty-Nine

I was sitting in my new recliner waiting for Harold when he returned from his afternoon walk. "Go get a drink of water then take a seat. I have news."

"Yes, ma'am," he said. After helping himself to water, he sat in his matching recliner. "What's up?"

"I talked with Niles today. The Russo Case is closed. Determined a suicide. And…" I paused for emphasis.

"And?"

"And Detective Warren abruptly retired, left his wife, and moved to Vietnam."

"He what?" Harold said in a loud voice.

"I know. Shocking, isn't it?" When Harold didn't comment further, I asked, "What do you think?"

"I think Warren stole the stash!"

Feeling like I wanted to jump out of my seat, I put the footrest down on my recliner. "What makes you say that?"

"No extradition policy," Harold replied, "that's what."

"What are you talking about and what does it have to do with Warren? Stop being so cryptic."

Harold set his glass down on the table between us. "Extradition is a legal process where one country or state surrenders an individual to another for legal proceedings. I happen to know that Vietnam has no formal extradition treaty with the United States."

"But Niles said he moved there because he suspects he might have step-siblings in the area. Plus, he was getting bored on desk duty, where he was placed when he returned from being on administrative leave."

Harold shook his head. "Kids of vets often think they have siblings in Vietnam. My bet is that he's using it as an excuse. Let's say he found jewels hidden in a container in Russo's apartment when he entered it the day Joey died. You did say Ethyl saw him as she was leaving Joey's apartment, right?"

"Yes. I believe she did."

"My guess is he didn't disclose his findings and pocketed the stash. He went about his investigation per usual for a few months, then something happened."

"You mean to cause him to be placed on administrative leave, then desk duty?"

Harold took another drink of water. "Yes. There's definitely something Niles isn't revealing to you about Warren. Perhaps we'll never find out but even if someone proved he stole the stash, now there's no recourse."

"You really think that's what happened? I always thought Warren was a bad egg, but THIS?"

"I'd bet money on it."

I got up and poured myself a Diet Dr. Pepper. I rarely drank soda, but this called for something stronger than water, and we were out of anything alcoholic. "So, all of the suspects, which now include Mable The Mole, by the way, are off the hook? They all were after the stash, but probably had nothing to do with Russo's demise?"

"That's the way I see it. What do you think?" Harold was good about asking for my opinion.

"I think you're right. I always doubted the premise that Joey was murdered. I even think he tossed his own apartment just to get attention and to make people think someone was after him. Joey would have been delighted if his murder were pinned on me, and Warren was just the man for the job. Thank goodness the case is closed and the detective is out of the picture. No more interrogations from him!"

Harold took our empty glasses to the sink. He looked over at me. "Now, can we settle down and spend our twilight years simply enjoying each other's company?"

"Yes, but first I have to make sure this story gets out so I can clear my name and get out of everyone's crosshairs."

"And you're just the woman to make that happen."

Getting up from my chair, I walked over to Harold. "Even though it probably wasn't meant to be one, I'll take that as a compliment. My dad always said, 'gossip is just news running ahead of itself in a red satin dress.'"

As I walked toward my bedroom, Harold called out, "You going to put on your satin dress?"

"Yes, Colonel. I am."

Questions for Discussion

1. What do you think of Martha getting married again? Given the opportunity, would you consider marrying at her age? Why or why not?

2. What are your feelings about residing in a senior living community? What are the advantages and disadvantages? Do you think Martha's life in assisted living is realistic?

3. Are you convinced that Joey committed suicide? Assuming there was a stash, do you think it was stolen by Detective Warren?

4. If you were in Martha's shoes, how would you stay engaged with life and as independent as possible?

5. What lessons can be learned from Ethyl and Martha's experience of burying the hatchet and becoming friends?

6. Martha seems to draw new friends to her like moths to a flame. Do you find it easy or hard to make new friends later in life?

7. Do you find yourself becoming more or less adventurous in life as you get older? Does reading about someone else's adventures make you want to get out more?

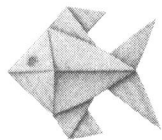

Acknowledgements

Once again, my team got the job done! A special thanks to Lynn Alexander my editor and proof reader extraordinaire. In my isolated world as an author, her expertise, encouragement, and friendship keeps me out of the paralyzing clutches of Mr. Doubt.

A book's cover acts as a silent salesperson, making the crucial first impression that attracts readers and signals the book's genre, tone, and content in seconds. Thanks to my cover and internal pages designer, Lance Buckley, for his continued commitment to helping my books make a good first impression.

Thank you to my BETA reader, Margaret Xanthopoulos.

Thanks to the real Sue Dalton, one of my biggest fans, for allowing me to use her name. I also want to acknowledge my new friend, Martha Raak, who resides in assisted living and is every bit as vibrant as fictional Martha. I met Martha after publishing my first book, *It's (Mostly) Good To Be Martha.* Getting to know her has shown me what life after ninety can be like and that "my" Martha is more authentic than I imagined.

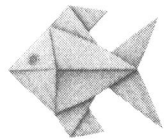

About the Author

MERSHON NIESNER, a Certified Life Coach, speaker, and newspaper columnist, found her calling as an author later in life. Her first book was published on her 75th birthday. Now in her eighties with five published books, Mershon is still going strong. Watch for *Winter Is In the Wind, Martyn Manor Mystery #3,* coming soon.

Mershon lives with her husband, Ken, in Naples, Florida. They have a blended family of six children, nineteen grandchildren, and eleven great-grands.

To subscribe to Mershon's monthly newsletter, Musings From Mershon, learn about upcoming events, and new book releases, visit **www.mershonniesner.com**. Mershon is available for book club events, book signings, and programs. For information, email her at **mershonniesner@gmail.com**.

Made in the USA
Coppell, TX
20 February 2026

71906127R10146